TREE BLACK

Connor de Bruler

MONTAG

For Mom and Courtney.

This novel wouldn't have come to fruition without Courtney's insights. I also want to thank everyone involved with the publication of this book. Lastly, I want to thank Watkin Tudor Jones and Yolandie Visser for all the spiritual momentum.

Connor De Bruler
Rock Hill, SC

"Kids run loose, buck-wild and unkempt.
This is a dream that I always have dreamt."
—*Jana Hunter*

"Cancer's at the door with a singing telegram."
—*William S. Burroughs*

CHAPTER ONE

The body drifted amid the reeds near the mouth of a steel culvert where the creek, otherwise distended by the falling rain, was reduced to a narrow trickle. Its soaked fur, turgid abdomen, and stiff extended legs brought the dog to a gradual slide along the bottom of the dark metal cave.

She wouldn't see it till morning. The rotting canine silhouette would be floating where the culvert emptied into a drainage ditch across from her bottom-floor apartment.

While the body dragged through the tunnel, Sandy lay awake in bed listening to the torrents beyond her prefab walls. Her bed was next to the only window in the room, which faced a 24-hour gas station. Separating the blinds with her fingers, she could see the neon beer logos burning like hot iron rods and reflecting off the slick pavement. The gutter had transformed into a small canal where a precession of cars exhausting their windshield wipers briefly hydroplaned as they raced down what would eventually become a lonesome country road. Sandy heard sirens nearly once a week and often endured the police cruiser's epileptic flashing into the early hours of the morning. She focused on the raindrops spattering against the window. The light that draped her upper body and part of her duvet cover was flecked with opaque smudges: shadows of the droplets on the glass. In the speckled, protracted light, her hair appeared a mild green from the Heineken logo and her face a dull red after the blinking neon Michelob sign. In plain light, her hair was a stark red and her skin a piano-key ivory. She flipped her pillow and rested against the cool side, staring at the rainy night. She saw an elderly woman clutching a brown paper bag and pink umbrella overhead as she crossed the street to the apartment complex. Sandy didn't recognize the woman. She didn't know most of her neighbors. Poor people were no longer social.

For an instant she could taste the rain. She could smell it. Somehow, she had left her own body and stepped onto the gritty, soaked curb beyond her window. It was something she didn't talk about, her ability to leave her own body. It was something that frightened her.

She reached for the side table and flipped her cell phone open to see the time. It was only two o'clock. If she fell asleep now, she would still have six hours. Nothing was going to happen. She sat upright on the dark half of the bed and eventually made her way to the bathroom, adjusting her panties. She flipped the light switch and allowed her pupils to adjust. Her bathroom did not reek of feminine odor and it never would. There was a bottle of generic Nyquil in the medicine cabinet offering an easy sleep in exchange for an uncomfortable, groggy morning. She poured a meager amount into the plastic cap and swigged the anise syrup.

Sandy Pogue ran the front desk at Palmetto Technical

College's machine shop and welding school. It was easy work and steady money. She found the position by accident after applying to be an ESL instructor. She had carved out a comfortable routine at Palmetto. The memories of past jobs were now collecting dust in the annals of her mind beside her bachelor's degree in Spanish with its faded calligraphy and cracked frame. She had once been a tour guide while living in Oaxaca, Mexico. She had also worked at a strip club which she no longer thought about.

Sandy was born in Charleston, South Carolina. The name on her birth certificate was not Sandy. It was legally changed when she turned twenty-three, six years ago. Her old name was not something she thought about either. Throwing things away was easy for her.

The gray panties stretched around her ankles as she dug her toes into the fibers of the pink rug. Sandy shifted atop the porcelain where she sat. The sound of rain normally lulled her to sleep. Caffeine would have to get her through tomorrow's workday if the effects of the Nyquil didn't wear off.

A memory that defied her acute will to forget surfaced. She was staying in the cheapest hotel she could find in Acapulco for a few days. The shabby room had water-damaged, peeling wallpaper. She saw the bed was stained with an even layer of crusty old blood, so she removed the sheets and bunched them in the corner. She nearly vomited upon entering the bathroom. It was not the bile-green color of the tile, the five 9-mm bullet holes in the wall or the iguana scuttling back outside through the open window, but the blue mass of flesh circling like a dead fish in the toilet. After the police took it away in a biohazard container, she discovered that she had been looking at a severed penis. She slept that night among las cucarachas.

Her cell phone lit up and began ringing. She pulled her underwear up and followed the blinking white light. She recognized the number.

"Hello?"

"I'm sorry for calling. Were you asleep?"

"No."

"Can't sleep either?"

"I just took something. I'll probably be able to now."

"You have sleeping pills?"

"No, I always take a thimble of Nyquil," she said.

"I heard that's not good for your liver."

"I don't take that much."

"Yeah," he sighed. "I've been listening to this book on tape about relaxation and meditating and that kind of stuff."

"Has it helped?"

"I play solitaire when I listen to it. The lady just drones on about stress and I tune it out. You know when you look at words and you don't really read them. I just hear her talk and I don't listen to any of it."

"I do that with music."

"It just fades into the background. I don't think people really die, they just fade into the background."

"You need to get some sleep, Yona," she said.

"Yeah, I'm sorry for bothering you."

"Was there any particular reason you called?"

"Oh, you know, just had to figure I weren't the only one on Earth tonight."

"You're not. I'll see you at work tomorrow."

"Yeah, I'll see you at work." She hung up and slowly set her phone back on the side table.

She fell face down on the neon green pillow and pulled the duvet over her body.

In her dream, she had a son. He eagerly sat at the kitchen table as she cooked pancakes. He was black. She cried each time he called her "mommy." They went to an art museum and then to a store where she bought him a miniature tuxedo. She spoke only Spanish, calling him mijo. The rest of the dream was spent trying to protect him from the gay porn on their television. She didn't understand why it was on every channel. The images of violent anal sex wouldn't go away even after she closed her eyes. The remote stopped working as she frantically pressed the buttons. Her son's well-being was at stake. She told him to run to his room. He looked at her and smiled. He said she didn't have to worry and he wasn't afraid. There was nothing to be afraid of. She didn't have to explain anything to him. He hugged her and they both walked outside to race tractors till nightfall.

CHAPTER TWO

Her landlord was a tall bearded man in his early fifties named Mr. Rice. He was usually kind and attempted to converse with his tenants, unlike his wife, Charlene, who screamed at mailmen. Mr. Rice went jogging each morning, regardless of the weather, in his white tracksuit. Sandy usually saw him through the window above her kitchenette sink as he jogged toward the park. Today he stood on the side of the drainage ditch with his hands in his pockets, staring into the dirty water. Sandy ate a small plate of scrambled eggs with ketchup and drank half a can of Dr. Pepper. When she cleaned off her dish, Mr. Rice was still standing near the drainage ditch. He stroked his mustache. The color had drained from his face. Sandy donned a pair of jeans, a hooded white sweater, and her pink retro sneakers. She walked into the morning fog, leaving her glass patio door ajar. Mr. Rice turned toward her with an insincere smile on his face. He didn't say anything.

"Good morning," she offered.

He cleared his throat. "Charlene didn't like Lucy, but I enjoyed having a dog in the house. I grew up with dogs on my dad's farm in Kentucky." As abruptly as he began, he fell silent, shuffling his feet in the wet grass.

She stepped over and looked at the Australian Shepherd's body in the drainage ditch as a swarm of gnats circled around the dull, open eyes. Lucy was an energetic, amiable dog. She was always gentle with the tenants' children who would pet her as she lay under the desk in the main office.

"How long had she been missing?"

"She took off last night," he said.

She helped Mr. Rice pull Lucy into a trash bag but she didn't have time to help him bury her. Sandy drove to work with the radio on thinking about his attachment to his dog. He would recuperate in a month or so and rescue another dog from the shelter; a smaller one he could keep indoors more often in spite of his wife's protests.

She took the highway to the adjacent county. It was a faster route but far less scenic.

She didn't have a designated parking spot like the instructors, but she never felt the need to kill anybody over it. The parking lot was empty half of the time anyway.

She walked from her car to the main door, noticing the young man in the Ford. Every morning, before getting to the welding class early, the same kid sat in his car with a cigarette, watching her enter the building. He looked directly into her eyes like he knew something. She tried not to notice him but couldn't. His stare was so fixed, so determined. If it weren't for Steve who unlocked the door for her, she would have felt threatened. Young men in the South had a way of giving harsh looks. It made them feel powerful.

It was the only blemish on her otherwise peaceful workday.

Officer Steve Lambert opened the entrance door for her as he did every morning with a Styrofoam cup of coffee in one hand.

"Howdy," he said before taking a sip. He wore his pants and utility belt above his navel.

"You got an interesting fact for me today, Steve?" she asked.

He bit his upper lip and thought for a moment. "Yeah, as a matter of fact I do." He pointed to his Taser and said, "This here Taser is a trademark unbeknownst to many people. But it's also an acronym. Stands for Thomas A. Swift's Electric Rifle or thereabouts. Company ripped it off on of them Tom Swift books if I'm not mistaken."

"Wow," she said. "You've outdone yourself this time."

"Bah, I'm an old man with nothing better." He walked away to begin his preliminary rounds on the campus.

Yona Bridger stood in the hallway feeding a wrinkled dollar to the vending machine. He was the same height as the machine and nearly as broad. Staff members with more seniority called him Ol' Bigfoot, though he was the youngest of the four welding instructors at just thirty-one years old. His name was the Cherokee word for "bear." He was raised by his grandparents in Brevard miles away from the reservation, and welded for Fluor-Daniel before an industrial accident left him with a limp and a sour taste in his mouth. He taught art students basic MIG skills at a private university in Asheville until transferring to Palmetto Technical College.

He was already wearing his welding cap and rawhide leather sleeves peppered in congealed metallic spatter.

"Sorry about calling last night," he said, tossing a spicy peanut to the back of his jaw.

"If I didn't want to talk to you I wouldn't have answered."

"Yeah, I guessed that. How are you doing?"

"My landlord's dog died. I helped him pull it out of a ditch this morning."

"That's a pretty morose start to the day. I'm sorry."

"I feel worse about my landlord. He really loved that dog. His wife didn't."

"She probably killed it." Yona had a stale sense of humor.

"She's uptight, but she isn't evil. He said the dog got out last night and by morning it was dead."

"How?"

"I guess it drowned. She wasn't old."

"What kind of dog."

"I think he said it was an Australian Shepherd. He got her from the Humane Society."

"I had a big German Shepherd on my grandpa's farm. We named him Waya. He was a rough soul."

"I never had any pets aside from my goldfish."

"Well, I hope you have a good day." He placed a hand on her shoulder. She noticed, once again, his religious stigmata. There were two identical scars on the palms of his hands. Apparently, as an eighteen-year-old welding student, a tungsten rod shattered under the automatic grindstone, partially crucifying him.

"You want to a get drink after?" she asked.

"I'll look forward to it," he said. "I gotta go cut some base metal for the rookies."

"Bye."

She headed to the front desk and clipped her nametag to her sweater. She logged onto the computer, deleting random e-mails. She thought about Lucy once more, and looked at the ceiling for two minutes. Then she had a short exchange with Gloria Saez, the custodian from Peru.

"Buenos días."

"Buenos días. ¿Todo el mundo feliz?" asked Gloria.

"Ojalá."

"Ojalá que tengas un buen día chica. Fuiste una oruga pero ahora eres una mariposa. Lo conozco."

Sandy usually found herself pondering Gloria's greetings.

CHAPTER THREE

Since she was three years old, Sandy grew up in apartments and town homes. She once lived beside an assisted living complex where she often spoke to the elderly and the mentally challenged. She remembered a young man in his early thirties exiled to a wheelchair after a car accident. His brain had sustained a significant amount of damage. He called himself Billy and often spoke other languages without noticing.

"Du have so ein bella face!" he would say. He also passed out origami flowers that took him hours to fold. People said he beat his girlfriend before the accident.

A quadriplegic man used to drive his breath-powered scooter down the sidewalk with his daughter holding onto on the back, kicking over trashcans.

Sandy made frequent, half-hearted attempts to run away from home. She would always find herself lost in the ominous darkness of the park where black silhouettes of ghosts silently walked across the vacant expanse of the jogging track and sat beside her on the cold bleachers. She watched shirtless men playing midnight games of basketball under the floodlights. Their tattoos offered fragments of life lessons and insights into the distant world of vulgarity and freedom. The rattle of the chain nets and the frenetic shuffle of feet provided the illusion of security as she lay in a bed of kudzu vines. The basketball players once allowed her to listen in on a free-style rap competition. She drank a plastic cup of purple Gatorade against her better judgment and made a couple free throws on the blacktop court when they finished.

Sandy was still apartment hopping as an adult. Her latest apartment was not large but the location was convenient. Her shower had been clogged for days. She finally bought a packet of sodium hydroxide and dumped the chalk-colored pellets into the drain. A blue froth erupted and the harsh sting of burning chemicals filled her nostrils and mouth causing her run to from the bathroom in a fit of coughing.

Yona finally rang her doorbell, holding a bottle of cheap Polish vodka in a brown paper bag. She unlocked the deadbolt and opened the door, still choking on the fumes.

"What's wrong?"

"Cleaning out my drain with chemicals."

He entered her apartment and set the bottle on the kitchenette counter. She pulled off his denim jacket and threw it in the closet. They walked into the bathroom and watched the drain pop and fizz, burning away the mass of hair and dead skin.

"Smells like vinegar," he said. "You know that drain cleaner can put you blind?"

"I figured."

Yona knelt down and sealed the packet and tucked it deep

inside the cabinet underneath the sink. He ran the bath water until the sizzling sodium hydroxide dissipated within the plumbing.

"Leave the door open so that smell goes away," she said. Sandy removed her sweater, revealing a black-laced tank top, and slid through the glass door to the patio to sit in her worn foldout chair. Yona took off his socks and stepped onto the warm concrete square.

"You got a smoke?"

"Of course," he said. He produced a pack of menthol Marlboros, pulled one out with his teeth, and flicked a cheap plastic Bic. Sandy reached for the cigarette and took a long drag. She puffed the smoke out the side of her mouth with a faint expression of guilt in her eyes as she handed it back to him.

Yona placed the cigarette in the side of his mouth and let the glowing ember wiggle as he spoke.

"That the ditch where you found the dog?" He pointed with his index finger.

"Yup."

"Shame."

She took the cigarette back and gave it a few more puffs. "You ever try marijuana when you were a kid?"

"Nah, I wasn't around those types of folks. Good ol' boys are drinkers."

"I hung out with hippies in college. I had a pink wig I wore all the time. I used to keep this clip in it for roaches when they got too short to hold."

"You liked going to your fancy four-year institution?" he asked, sarcastically.

"I think it was necessary for a person like me."

"Did you always speak Spanish?"

She thought for a moment and tossed the half smoked cigarette into the wet lawn. "Come on, let's go make some screwdrivers."

They walked back inside and shut the glass door behind them and closed the large white blinds. Sandy pulled a carton displaying Donald Duck's smiling image out of the fridge and liberally poured the vodka into two water glasses before lightly dusting the tops with orange juice. Yona looked at the carton for a while.

"It's kinda weird that he'd be smiling. I always found cartoon ducks to be rather unsavory characters. Donald was always hesitant and slow to trust. Daffy Duck, from the Looney Tunes, was a money-grubbing backstabber."

"You over-think everything." She took a giant slug of her screwdriver. "God, I hate the way cigarettes make my hair smell."

"You and me should stop smoking."

"Yeah, I figure," she said. "Isn't there a phobia of ducks?"

"I think there's a really strange phobia. A phobia that somewhere a duck is constantly watching you." He sipped his drink and gasped. "Only you could make trailer-park screwdrivers like these."

She smacked his ass and retreated to the living room couch.

"You never answered my question."

"Which one?"

"Did you always have a knack for Spanish?"

"No," she said. "I failed my first year of Spanish in seventh grade had to retake the class."

"When did you get into it?"

"When I met a very sad Colombian named Señor Plata. He was the Spanish instructor my sophomore or junior year in high school. I can't remember which one. He was a short, feeble man. A good teacher, but no authority, you know? He was more than a pushover; he was a punching bag for those All-American football jackasses who wanted a fiesta every goddamned day. They had no respect for this poor guy, coming out of all that violence and corruption and chaos of the time. I mean you could tell this guy had some mileage on him the way he would speak so quietly and yet so sincerely. The first day of the semester this guy shakes every single student's hand as they enter the classroom. He'd just stare directly into your eyes and tell you that he was very glad to have you in his class. And you fucking knew he wasn't just saying it to say it. He meant something. He was one of the few people I'd met growing up who meant what they said, who put their heart into their words. And they tortured him. By the end of the term, they put a tack in his seat and called him a wetback and did all their presentations on the cartels. It was hard to go to that class every day.

"Eventually, Powder Puff is in full swing and the cheerleaders convince him to put on a tutu and lace fairy wings. They set him up with a pair of roller-skates and have him skid down the halls to collect money for the charity or whatever cause we were funding."

"Why did he agree?"

"They convinced him it wasn't against the rules to skate through the halls during free period."

"No, why would he let them humiliate him further?"

"Everybody was dressing weird during Powder Puff. I guess he wanted to fit in. I just remember seeing him skating along in the tutu with the collection jar under his arm, waving a popsicle-stick wand dipped in glitter. And that was it. That was evil triumphing over good for me. He had lost. He had completely lost to those fuckers. I don't know why but watching him lose made me pursue Spanish."

"Damn, Sandy."

They drank for a little while longer.

"How about you? Why'd you go into welding?"

"I did a lot of crap here and there during high school, and my grades suffered as they often do for working kids. It just seemed like that was what you had to do. I come from a background of poor-ass Indians. Working was life. I saw being a journeyman as a great thing. I got into an apprenticeship with Fluor welding and ended up loving it. I mean I had to get my eye worked on after a spec of metal from the grinder ricocheted. That was before full-face shields were mandatory. Doc moves in with a drill and then coats your eye in goop then you gotta wear an eye patch for two weeks. Then, of course, the tungsten rod shattered when I was doing TIG, went through my hands. But none of that scared me. I thought it was part of the business. After my two year contract was up working for them in the field, I signed back on. Finally my leg got fucked up and I said, 'To hell with this shit.' I took the money from the settlement and went to the association to become an instructor."

"I hear you're a good teacher, Yona," she said.

"I try to convey to the boys that welding is an art and art is spiritual. If you love welding, you can find solace in it. I think they appreciate that. I'm also a stickler for safety." Yona was on the verge of slurring his words. He set the screwdriver on the coffee table.

"You ever had a power drill?" she asked him.

"The hell?"

"You know a screwdriver is vodka and orange juice? Well, a power drill is Everclear and grapefruit juice."

"That's sounds god awful, Sandy."

"I just came up with that. I thought it was smart." She unbuttoned her bra and took her pants off. There was a small black tattoo on her right hip. Yona leaned toward her on the couch and rested his head in her lap. She stroked his hair.

"What was stripping like?" he asked

"I was more of a showgirl than a stripper," she said. "It was a Goth club. People wore capes and leather, that kind of crap. Manson and Rob Zombie blasted from the speakers. I used to crawl out on stage like a zombie while 'American Witch' or 'Sweet Dreams' played and the strobe lights were blinking."

"Did you use a fake name?"

"Of course. I was Morticia."

"From the Addams Family?"

"Oh, yeah. They ate that shit up."

They both laughed. Sandy stroked his hair a little longer before kissing him. He took off her tank top and carried her into the bedroom. She stretched backwards, extending her stomach and curling her legs till her feet nearly touched her head. She raised her hands upward and unbuckled his belt. His pants fell to the floor with a metallic thud as the buckle hit the carpet.

"I'm not pretty naked," he said.

"Sure, you are."

He sat on the bed and pulled his shirt off. They embraced each other and kissed a few times. The memory of the workday had drowned in vodka. Yona felt himself finally relax as the stiffness in his bad leg and neck left his body.

"I'm gonna fall asleep," he said.

"Not on my watch."

CHAPTER FOUR

The ashtray, built into the top of the garbage receptacle, had retained the water from the rainy nights. The remaining nubs of cigarettes floated in the stagnant murk like drowned caterpillars. Mr. Rice hauled the giant cylinder to the edge of the curb and emptied it into the storm drain, then refilled the ashtray with a bag of khaki-colored sand. He locked the entrance to the main office with his ring of keys and took the sandbag back to the maintenance shed: a dark gazebo-shaped structure across from the pool. He set the bag near the mop and bucket and locked the creaky door. As he turned around a burst of adrenaline shot through his body like an electrical current. A thick rat snake slithered past him through the chain-link fence and back into the woods.

"Damn it." He stopped for a moment and caught his breath, sitting down in one of the plastic chairs. A truck passed on the road beyond apartments. The pool water refracted the glare from the moon as well as the light from the underwater lamps. Angelic bands of soft ethereal light drifted across the surface of his body and the edges of the concrete. He sat alone, thinking.

There was a rustling in the bushes on the other side of the fence accompanied by the brief patter of bare feet running across the asphalt. Mr. Rice stood up and pulled out his compact LED flashlight from his pocket. In the past, his wife Charlene had spotted a group of teenagers skinny-dipping in the pool at some ungodly hour of the morning. She called the police-a classic overreaction on her part-but they were long gone before the lone officer pulled into the apartment's cul-de-sac. She said there were three blonde white-girls and one very young black-boy. Mr. Rice didn't like calling the police for anything. As a youth, he and a group of friends had spiked their root beers with stolen gin. They drank and smoked near the abandoned movie house where a cop had questioned them. They told him they were drinking root beer and crassly offered him a taste. He took a swig and immediately tasted the gin.

"There's gin in this here root beer."

"Well, if that were true then you'd have to admit to drinking on the job, 'cause ya can't smell no gin from the bottle. You might as well run along deputy and do that misconduct of yours somewhere else."

The officer pulled out his baton and struck several of the young men in across the face, kicking them in the throat as well. He chased them across the empty parking lot until he was nothing but a dark outline in the distance, catching his breath. One of Mr. Rice's friends had a bicuspid knocked out that night.

He walked across the pool as quietly as possible. When he reached the edge of the gate, he switched the flashlight on. There was nothing in the bush or the road beyond the gate. If there were any kids out tonight, they had probably seen him and decided against using the facilities. He headed back to his apartment and thought of Lucy once more. Lucy was buried under the Willow Path Apartments' entrance sign in a worn suitcase beneath several petunias.

He walked into his town home and tossed his keys on the counter. A massive pile of unpaid bills and notices from the city had been neatly stacked near Lucy's jar of dog treats. He stepped into the entranceway closet and parted the coats as if they were a curtain, grabbing the first thing he saw before walking into the bedroom.

Charlene was dressed in a nightgown, reading a gardening magazine. He stared at her as she sat upright on their bed.

"Charlene?"

"Yes?"

"Do you want to go skinny-dipping in the pool?"

"No," she said as she turned the page.

"Of course not," he mumbled. "Did you let Lucy out last night and not tell me?"

"No. A million times no. I'm sorry about the dog," she said without looking up from the magazine, keeping his frame in her peripheral vision. "What are you holding?"

There was a short pause as he stood over her.

"Charlene."

"What?"

"Goodbye." He lifted the double-barrel shotgun and fired it through the magazine and into her chest. Her body was propelled backward against the wall eventually falling sideways, knocking over the lamp on her side drawer. The white sheets and the wall behind the bed were stained with blood. The weight of her body crushed the light bulb from the lamp against the floor. Everything went dark. He broke the shotgun over his forearm and tossed the empty shell onto the rug.

CHAPTER FIVE

Yona and Sandy sat on the edge of her driveway watching the police roll tape across the entrance of the Rice's doorway. The cul-de-sac had become a theater in which every tenant took a seat. They watched patiently until the body bags were brought outside.

"Should we ask what happened?"

"No. They wouldn't tell us," said Yona. "Isn't it obvious what happened?"

"Not to me it isn't."

"Who do you pay rent to next month?"

"Shut up." She looked to her right and saw a couple crying, holding each other. "This doesn't make any sense." Sandy walked across the road. A young officer in a dark-blue uniform and a high and tight, military-style haircut raised his hand to prevent her from coming any closer.

"Ma'am, you can't come any further."

"What happened to Mr. and Mrs. Rice?"

"I can't tell you that."

"Please, I'm their friend. I need to know."

"I'm not authorized to say. Please step back across the street."

Sandy stepped backward, looking at the young officer. The crying couple approached her and asked what had happened.

"I don't know," she said.

They left her alone.

She looked up at the black, starless sky and walked away. Yona followed her into the house. They lay in bed together, pulling up the covers.

"How did you get your name?" she asked him.

"My grandma told me that my mother was very fond of bears. A black bear wandered into the yard one day when my mom was pregnant with me. It stared at her for a while but didn't come any closer. It walked away, wasn't interested in anything my mom had. She thought the bear had spared her, so she gave me the name."

Yona's mother died while giving birth. His father was a truck driver from Montana who had left before she knew she was pregnant. He never met either of them.

"Can I ask you a personal question?" He stroked her cheek with the back of his thick hand.

"Yes."

"What was your birth name?"

She closes her eyes.

He regretted asking the question.

"It was Seth. Seth Leary Pogue," she said. "A very Irish name, as my parents put it."

"Were your folks Irish?"

"They were Catholics. My dad was Irish. My mom's maiden

name was Purser. I think her great-grandparents were German. They both said they were Irish Catholics. I think it gave them a sense of identity. They weren't that religious really."

"Are they still alive?"

"Yes, but they don't want to talk to me. I haven't spoken to them since college. They stopped talking to me when I was moonlighting at the club to pay for everything. After the initial transition, I went to Mexico for a while. I'm pretty sure they still think I'm down there."

"You mentioned a sister in Tennessee a while back."

"Yeah, I have an older sister. She's a dental assistant. She just had a baby girl."

"What's your sister's name?"

"Aileen."

"Do you have a good relationship with her?"

"Yeah, she's been shopping with me. She didn't understand at first but once I went on hormones and started passing, she accepted it. I mean, she was encouraging and sweet the whole time, but she didn't really understand until I went on HRT. I talk to her a lot. She always knew what to say."

"I'm sorry about your folks," he said.

"I've been over it for a while."

"Did you dress up like a girl when you were in school?"

"No. When I was a really young kid, I used to sit in the grass and close my eyes. I could see myself with pigtails and a dress. When I got older, like when I was a teenager, I used to lie in bed and envision myself with boobs and a pussy. I didn't start experimenting with different clothes until I was finishing high school. I wore really flashy stuff."

"I wasn't much of a crazy guy in my school days," he said.

"No, you were too busy getting maimed."

"True."

She set her hand against his face. "Do you ever worry about what the guys at work will think if they knew about us and what I am?"

"Do you ever worry?"

"Yes," she said. "I'm always afraid."

"I'm not afraid. My business is my business. I mean, what do they care? I'm not 'one of the guys.' I'm just the young Indian with a limp: Ol' Bigfoot."

"I pass well and I'm attracted to men, so I'm lucky," she said.

"Oh yeah, don't lesbians hate Trans people or something?"

"I wouldn't know. None of my friends are lesbians."

"I think you dwell too much on the bad things and not enough on what's good," he said.

"You're right. My landlords just died. I should seek the silver lining."

"Well, sarcasm ain't gettin' you nowhere."

They lay in pure silence. She wrapped her hand around his shoulder as he shifted to his side. She thought about Mr. Rice and the apparent monotony of his daily life. He jogged every morning, and then made a few rounds with the maintenance man, Theodore, until finally sitting behind the desk in the main office for the remainder of the day. Charlene was indoors unless she was verbally abusing the mailman or an unfortunate tenant. She saw her scream at a mailman once for harming a fragile package. He puttered along in the anonymous white truck, ignoring her, whistling as though it would dispel her poison.

She would learn about the details tomorrow night if she decided to watch television. People were killed every day in apartment complexes, according the local ten o'clock news. She did not own a television but the faculty at Palmetto Tech normally kept a couple of televisions on in the recreation rooms behind the machine shop.

"Who has to die on a Friday night?" she said out loud.

"You gotta go sometime," Yona mumbled.

There was a knock at the door early in the morning. Yona answered it, standing in his polka dot boxers and grease-stained t-shirt.

"Hello, sir. Have you been saved?" They stood in the doorway: two young men of equal height wearing sleeveless, button-up shirts and black clip-on ties.

"There's no soliciting in apartment complexes."

"We're not selling anything."

"Yes, but you're soliciting for a church and that's still illegal."

"There's nothing illegal about knocking on someone's door and engaging in neighborly conversation."

Yona stepped outside and pulled the door shut behind him. "You're not my neighbor. You're my enemy. Your forefathers took my land, raped my people, and still had the gall to shoot at my brothers at Wounded Knee in 1973. Now you come to my door and you break another law to conform me to your beliefs. I won't stand for it."

The two young men didn't speak. They couldn't tell whether or not he was serious. Yona stepped past them and rifled through the bed of his Toyota pickup. He pulled the leather safety guard off his hatchet and held it to his side.

"We scalp y'all where I come from," he said.

Both young men ran away down the road. Yona tossed the hatchet back into the truck and walked inside. Sandy was cooking eggs on the skillet.

"Religious witnesses?"

"I scared 'em off with the Indian gambit."

"I should have told them I was a witch or something," she said. "I could draw a pentagram on the wall."

They ate in the living room with their feet propped up on the coffee table.

"I've come to find there are three effective methods to getting holy rollers off your doorstep," said Yona. "Show 'em a hatchet. Show 'em a gun. Offer 'em a blowjob."

"Some of them might appreciate a blowjob."

"It depends," he said. "If you offer it straight-faced, they normally run away. Sometimes you catch a bad egg who's all in. That's very rare."

"I don't know. One thing I learned about working in a strip club is that more people are down for weird shit that you'd think."

"Did you guys have a fetish room in the back or something?"

"Nothing that strange. There were magazines sold in the lobby. I saw some bizarre crap."

"Like what?"

"Whips, chains, coke cans...I could go on."

"You didn't like working there did you?"

"It paid."

"That's not my question."

"Well...I guess I hated it. Toward the end, I really hated it. It just wasn't me. There was too much vice, too many sad stories, and..."

"And what?" he asked.

"That's about all I can think of," she said. "You want the yolk hard or runny."

"You know I like 'em runny."

"Here." She lifted the skillet off the stove and slapped the egg onto his plate with the spatula. She cracked another egg and poured herself half a glass of Donald Duck orange juice.

"Where did you get that Donald Duck stuff," he asked.

"City Grocery. The cheap place." She watched him dip his toast in the yellow egg yolk.

"What was shopping like in Mexico?"

"More or less the same. They have big stores in the larger cities, but if you go into the pueblos the shelves can look pretty bare. You buy what they got."

"What does a Mexican eat for breakfast?"

"Most people I knew had coffee, toast, and fresh cheese," she said. "Kids would drink fresh-squeezed juice or milk."

Yona wiped his face with a napkin. "You ever think about going back."

"Never."

"Never?"

"I honestly think a lot about moving out West."

"California? Arizona?"

"Oregon."

"What's in Oregon?"

"I don't know," she said.

CHAPTER SIX

Yona showed up for work early Monday morning. He and Sandy never drove together. He normally came in through the back entrance between the massive Argon and Acetylene tanks. He liked to see who the really dedicated students were. They'd be grinding off the oxidized surfaces or running beads on their own base metal. Before he entered the building, he saw somebody was already in the yard. A stocky kid with blonde hair named Thompson plunged the metal slab into the cooling tank with his vise grips. The steam rose above the water as he propped the handle against the side of the rusted tank. He removed his gloves and sat down next to the scrap metal yard, stuffing a teaspoon's worth of Kodiak chewing tobacco into the corner of his straight, viper-like jaw.

"What are you doing?"

"Practicing," he said, giving Yona a cheeky smile.

"Who let you in?"

"Derek was testing out the new plasma cutter. I just told him I wanted to run some beads before class. That alright?"

"Yeah, that's fine."

Yona walked into the back of the shop. Derek Larson was dicing a pipe into segments with the plasma cutter. He turned off the machine and flipped the shield above his face.

"How was your weekend, Ol' Bigfoot?"

"A bit strange," he said. "That kid Thompson's in here running beads ain't he?"

"He's using his own base metal. I don't figure it to be such a bad thing at all. Kid's got some talent."

"How are we doing on rods?"

"He doesn't use but one or two."

"Alright. If he starts going overboard, you make sure to lock him out of the shop before class starts."

Yona walked into the lounge and poured himself a coffee in a Styrofoam cup. He stretched out over the couch. Harold walked in and set his bagel in the refrigerator.

"What's up Bigfoot?"

"Nothing. I didn't know you were coming in today."

"Yeah, I ain't much for the hospital. Once I could walk okay, I didn't figure I needed to sit around the house neither."

Harold, the oldest instructor at sixty-three years old, wore a thick moustache that obscured his lips and shaved his wrinkled skull clean of any hair.

"What'chu end up in the hospital for?" Yona asked.

"Passing the stones my friend."

"No shit?"

"I shit you not. It was like pissing a box of razorblades," he said. "I pulled out the stint by accident. Thought my dick was gonna come off with it."

"Now why the hell would you pull the stint out?"

Harold straightened his back and coughed into the side of his arm. "Well, a nurse come up into the hospital room and said, 'We got to get you to pissing. Make sure everything's alright.' She hands me a damn mason jar and I whip out my equipment and piss for her. I did it alright, but there was a small stitch hanging out of my dick. Now what were the chances that I'd get my thumb caught in there?"

"Holy shit," said Yona, massaging the bridge of his nose.

"Shit is right. I pull the thing out and the nurse just looks at me. She gets the doctor to come up and he's just smiling. I say, 'I done pulled it out.' And he's like, 'Yep, ye dern did.' That was that."

"It didn't ruin your plumbing?"

"Doctor said it was just there to facilitate urination. I'd be fine either way."

"My God. That's a story alright."

Harold wiped his moustache. "Well, I gotta clock in."

"I'll see you 'round, man."

They shook hands and Harold walked away.

At 8 o'clock, Yona limped into the classroom, took attendance, and began class. His students seemed amused by his presence today. He couldn't understand why. They were combative and crass. His classes were typically a breeze, but something had faltered. He stood on the edge of the welding shop and they were content staying in their booths. No one approached him with a question or a sample of their work for critique. At 11:30 the young men punched their cards and dispersed for lunch. Yona headed into the lounge where Sandy was unfolding the tinfoil on a burrito. He sat down next to her and pulled off the top of a Tupperware container filled with red beans and rice.

"How are you?" he asked.

"I watched the morning news," she said. "There was nothing about Mr. Rice." She was pale and her eyes looked red.

"You don't look so good, Sandy."

"Something's been on my mind." Her hands were shaking.

Yona's heart dropped into his chest.

"What's going on, Sandy? What happened to Mr. Rice?"

"This has nothing to do with my landlord," she said and choked a little. "I'm having a panic attack. I'm afraid of what you might do."

"You're not making any goddamn sense, Sandy. Just tell me."

"There's a kid, Yona. He's here every morning. He's one of yours. He could always see it in me."

"You're scaring me," he said.

"Yona, I'm stealth. I'd lose my job if they found out about me... and us."

"That's not the world me live in anymore, Sandy."

"Yes it is. Yes it is. He threatened me, Yona. This blonde kid, he's been looking at me from his car every morning as I enter the building. He threatened to tell on me, Yona. He's seen us together." Sandy was crying.

Yona stood up. She tried to stop him but he pushed her away and she collapsed face down on the table. He walked out of the lounge and headed toward the lunch hall. Harold passed him and gave him a brief pat on the back. Yona did what he could to smile. Everyone in the room seemed to be watching him, taking in every movement he made. It was mutiny. He made his way to the middle of the hall and found Thompson sitting with two other young men of equal height and stature. He wasn't eating, but playing cards with a wad of tobacco in his lip.

"Thompson."

"Yeah?"

"I gotta talk to you about something real quick."

"Sure thing. What's up?"

"Let's go outside," he said.

They sat down on the smoking bench. Everyone was watching.

"What the fuck did you say to Sandy, Thompson?"

He hesitated and choked on his own words. "I...I just said what we all ought to feel 'bout somebody lying 'bout who they are." He found his courage after staring back at his peers through the glass doorway and windows. "I mean, Jesus Mr. Bridger. You know Sandy's a man."

"How are you sure?"

"I've heard talk."

"You've only heard talk."

"I heard you and her talk. Y'all said enough and did enough." he said. "I always knew something was funny about her face. Now, I know. She's a man."

"No, she's not. Not anymore."

"That doesn't mean nothing. The hell he is. Ain't nothing to it."

"You don't know a lot, kid. You're ignorant. You've been raised ignorant. Folks around you are ignorant. That's all you know. My personal life is my own. You don't fuck with it."

"The hell, man? I looked up to you. We all did. But you're just a faggot degenerate, sticking your cock up some tranny's corn hole."

"You don't have to respect me, Thompson, but you cannot threaten Sandy."

"I don't think so. I'm gonna show the school and ya'll will be in a fix," he said threateningly.

"Why don't you be a real man and settle your beef yourself you coward little prick?"

Thompson spat a wad of tobacco juice in Yona's face. Everyone was silent. Yona unfolded a paper towel from his pocket and cleaned his face. Thompson stood before him, waiting for something.

"You think we're gonna fight?" asked Yona. "Nah, that's too easy. I'm gonna walk inside and I'm gonna go about my day because I'm better than a little pecker like you. And you are gonna get expelled for blackmailing an instructor."

"That might be, but I already got the president my pictures of ya'll in the parking lot. You're both getting sacked for misconduct."

Yona turned to Thompson and crushed his nose with a swift blow from his left fist. There was blood on the concrete and his t-shirt. He writhed on the ground, screaming.

Yona instantly regretted everything.

CHAPTER SEVEN

She was breastfeeding kittens. There were ten kittens huddled together in the bottom of the storm drain. Her father used a jack to remove the concrete top, so he could kneel down inside the drain and, one by one, hand them to Sandy as she set their weightless bodies into a cardboard box lined with bath towels. The kittens whined as they crawled on top of one another, smearing feces into their fur. She bathed them in the kitchen sink and fed them with her sister, Aileen. They allowed the kittens to latch onto their chests while they dribbled milk on their shirts. The kittens sucked from the milk-soaked fibers as if they were breastfeeding. It was the closest she had ever come to being a mother.

She beat up a boy at school for saying he used to tie bottle rockets to kitten's heads and watch them explode mid-air. She didn't believe him, but the idea was enough to set her off. Sandy was a boy at that time and dressed no different from any other ten-year-old. She had a crew cut and shirts displaying the images of

Batman, the Power Rangers, and the Ninja Turtles. The boy she attacked for his morbid comment did his best to fight back, giving Sandy a bloody nose, but she cornered him against the monkey bars until a teacher pulled them apart. She was dragged by the collar of her Batman shirt into the principal's office.

"Why exactly did you attack Robert?" he asked, sitting behind his desk.

"He said he killed kittens."

"Did he really say that?"

"Yes, he did," she pleaded. "He said he blew them up with fireworks."

"Seth, tell the truth."

It was there in the principal's office that she realized the pain she would have to feel for the rest of her life: the pain of being alone with the truth. The faint remnant of bloody-nosed, ten-year-old Seth Leary Pogue, the protector of helpless animals, lingered within her as she collapsed onto the floor, wondering why she had lost her job.

Yona had also lost his job that day.

Sandy awoke on her kitchenette floor enduring a migraine as she clutched the neck of a decidedly half-empty bottle of vodka. The 11 o'clock radio news had finally released the information that Mr. Rice had shot himself shortly after murdering his wife. The program quickly cut to a soft story about an elderly man who made antique canoes in the Upstate. Only moments before, she was issued a notice that unless she intended to buy her apartment from the city, she would have no choice but to relocate since the Rices had been evading taxes and municipal regulations for almost two years.

She pulled herself across the carpet, leaving her bottle to bleed out its remaining contents on the linoleum, and escaped into the unwashed sheets of her queen-sized bed. She had fallen on her face. A warm trickle of blood coated her lips. She would always be another variation of the same ten-year-old boy with a bloody nose. She sniffled and walked into the bathroom. Her nose didn't look broken. She had mostly likely burst a vessel. She retreated back to her bed and fell asleep.

She awoke to the sound of the doorbell. Her room was illuminated by the neon beer logos across the street. It was night. Her migraine had dissipated into a fairly tolerable headache.

"Please open the door, Sandy."

"Go away," she said, weakly. There was no way Yona could have heard her.

"Sandy, let me talk to you."

"Go away." Her arms were shaking and she found it difficult to open her eyes.

In her dream she could fly, but not without effort. The air was thick and she had the ability to pull herself up into the sky as if she were swimming. She was taking a trip across the United States, heading north toward Baltimore. There, she encountered an old friend from college. Nadya was a black girl with purple hair and a Chinese dragon tattooed around her arm. Nadya allowed her to stay at her dilapidated house with her roommates for a night. They lived in a neighborhood with a dangerous gang of roaming street children who spat mouthfuls of kerosene at passersby before flicking matches at them. Nadya's roommates, who were all youthful hippies, advised Sandy to carry a bottle of water to dilute the kerosene in case the children ever spat on her. When she left to go west, to Portland, Oregon, she was corned by the children in an abandoned industrial park. She pulled herself into the air before the kerosene could touch her and flew away into a purple sunset, excited for what she might discover on the West Coast. She thought about moving to Colorado or Oregon when she initially decided to transition, but she ended up taking a guide job in Mexico.

When she was eighteen, she stole a black dress from her sister's closet and waxed her entire body in the bathtub at her pot dealer's house. His name was Ricardo. His girlfriend, Angelica, did her makeup and showed her how to stuff a bra. Sandy put on a pink wig and fake ear and nose rings she bought from a Halloween store. Instead of attending prom night, she went to a gay bar with Ricardo and Angelica after smoking expensive hashish joints in their Volkswagen van. The music was loud and the strobe lights blurred the dancing crowds' features. She could feel the throbbing bass inside her chest. Older women were asking her to dance. She blushed, realizing how well she passed as a woman. She won a pole-dancing contest and stood on stage thanking the emcee as he set a plastic tiara over her pink hair. A tall young man wearing a Hawaiian t-shirt bought her a few tequila shots and asked her if she was a lesbian. He couldn't see through her thick makeup and blood-red lipstick. She told him she was straight. They went to the bathroom where she saw a couple of Ricardo's regulars snorting cocaine. He took his pants off in the stall and she began to caress his penis with her tongue. After a few minutes of oral sex, he forced her head away with formidable strength and grabbed onto her thighs. She held onto the toilet seat to prevent her head from dunking into the dirty bowl. Her tiara slid off and splashed into the water. The muffled sound of the techno music permeating the walls seemed to grow louder as Sandy felt her stomach churn. She realized what was about to happen. She was still wearing plaid, men's boxers underneath her dress. He lowered them to her knees without comment, lubricated his penis with spit, and jammed on through her rectum. It didn't feel good at all. Her skin stung as though it were ripped. She clenched as best she could. There seemed to be nothing preventing her from defecating everywhere. Her head was shoved into the side of the toilet when she began to cry. He pulled out after twenty-minutes and wiped the shit off the head of his penis with a square of toilet paper and let it flutter down into the water, spreading on top of her tiara. She rested her head on the seat sobbing the makeup away. She would never forget what he had said before walking out: "Dude, get over it."

CHAPTER EIGHT

The tall grass and dandelions whipped against the wooden steps in the faint breeze. Harold sat on the modest porch next to the cooler filled to the brim with steadily melting ice and cracked open another Tecate. The screen door slammed as Yona limped back outside. He eased into his worn fold-out chair and lit a cigarette, returning the lighter and the soft pack of menthol Marlboros to the lone breast pocket of his green t-shirt. Yona's trailer stood in the clearing of a vast expanse of kudzu. To the left was a road of red clay shaped by the tread of his truck tires.

Harold took a sip of beer. "Doctor said when I got the chance I better have me a few beers. Said it would flush out my system." Harold shook his can of beer and watched it froth.

"Water would probably do you better and help out your circulation, too." Yona tapped his ash.

There was a long silence as Yona stared at the greenery before them.

"I appreciate you sticking by me, Harold."

"It isn't hard. Everybody knew a little shit like Thompson had it coming. Didn't have no right. I were you, I'd have whipped the living hell out of him. They'd have fired me on the spot instead of slip me some measly severance check like they did you. They shouldn't have done you like that, man."

"I punched him. That was that. But they threw Sandy out because of who she is. There isn't any sense to it."

"You're too young to remember. When I was your age, they'd have done her in a lot worse."

"She was so scared, Harold, but I just didn't see it coming. It just barreled us over in a few moments."

"That's how it was when Mark died. He was never quite the overachiever like his sister, but I didn't think he'd die. You're gonna come back from this crap. I promise you," he said. "The rest of the guys, they're cowards Yona. They're too afraid to stand up. As far as they're concerned, you're gay."

Yona stretched his arms with the cigarette hanging in his mouth. "I believe you. I seriously do, but I just can't figure what I'm gonna do now. Sandy's barred herself away from me for the past two days. She won't answer the door when I knock. Do you think she resents me for rocking the boat?"

"You didn't rock the boat. None of this would have happened if Thompson hadn't been scheming the whole time."

"I can't stop thinking about her and I can't stop thinking about where I want to go from here. You know? What am I gonna do for a job? I just can't bring myself to go back to construction."

"You'll find something. I got a friend at a custom shop. They could use a guy with your skill." Harold took a sip and wiped the beer off his moustache with the back of his hand.

"Hell man, I'd appreciate it if you hooked me up with a number."

"I can do better. I'll give him your number and a recommendation."

Yona became calmer and he eventually stubbed out his cigarette and opened a Mexican beer.

"Trust me. You'll go back to work. Right now, you need to just chill out and get your head straight. Give Sandy a few days to herself. Don't go banging on her door again. She needs time to cool."

"I think I'll go home to get my head clear, away from this goddamned trailer."

"Back to the reservation?"

"No, I grew up in Transylvania County, North Carolina. My grandparents raised me on a farm. It isn't too far from Brevard."

"I wouldn't know it," said Harold. "You lived with your grandparents?"

"My mom didn't make it in childbirth."

"Yeah, that wadn't uncommon back in the day," he said. "What was she supposed to be like?"

"My grandma didn't talk about her much and my granddad never said anything about anything. I guess I never did know. It's hard to determine from the little tidbits I was left with whether she was a traditional Indian or plain strange."

"Who was your dad if you don't mind my asking."

"My dad might have been some truck driver from out West but I never gave a damn."

"Truck driver? He an Indian?"

"Nope."

"I didn't know you were half-white."

"Yep."

"What did ya'll raise on the farm?"

"Sheep. Half my life was shearing wool till I was 15."

"They still running the place?"

"No, they died a ways back. Left me the house. There hasn't been sheep on that farm in seven years."

"I'm sorry about that."

"I've made my peace with it." Yona took another sip of beer. "It's beautiful country up there."

"You got a damn farm home up northward just waitin' for you. That's convenient."

"I guess so. Thing's been paid off too."

Harold leaned back and patted the top of his bald head.

"What were you're folks like?" asked Yona.

Harold smirked. "Well, in America there's three kinds. You got the red, white, and blue: white collar, blue collar, and redneck. We must've been somewhere in between the blue and the red. My folks weren't as poor as most. They worked in a mill in Greenville. Everything was provided by the mill. It was like being in the army I guess. Daddy didn't drink. Mother went to church. It was all so serene. I came to find when I was older about all the riots and union problems but I was a baby during that time. My dad kept his job, so I figured he was never union. They were simple people, nothing special. I saw the real world once I joined the Marines."

"You were a Marine?"

"Oh, yeah. That's how I first started welding."

"That makes sense."

A car was approaching from the far end of the road. Yona and Harold sat trying to look relaxed in spite of the nervous anticipation. Sandy parked at an oblique angle beside Yona's pickup and casually stepped outside.

Yona could see the backseat of her car was filled with belongings.

He took another sip of beer.

Sandy didn't step onto the porch. Instead, she stood in the grass with her car keys in hand, looking at the two men from behind the shade of her sunglasses.

"I'm sorry I didn't answer the door," she said.

"You worried me," said Yona.

"I know." She took the glasses off and hung them on the collar of her shirt. "Mr. Rice shot himself after shooting his wife."

Harold seemed uneasy and confused. Yona filled him in about Sandy's landlords.

"I was evicted because he wasn't paying taxes. The city took the property back," she said.

"Jesus Christ." Yona threw his head back and massaged the bridge of his nose. "You're welcome to stay with me as long as you need."

"Thank you."

She finally sat down on the warped panel steps of the porch.

"You want a beer?"

"I don't drink beer."

The three of them sat in silence and watched a pair of buzzards circling in the distance. As twilight approached, Harold stood up and said he better be getting on, taking his cooler of melted ice and floating cans of beer to his SUV.

Sandy and Yona went inside and watched several cartoon comedy shows before going to bed.

The glare from a low moon spread across them like a thin sheet of wax paper. She watched one of Yona's cigarettes smolder in a blue-crystal ashtray on the windowsill. The mechanical hum of an AC unit syncopated with the squawk of several night birds and chirruping cicadas and crickets, forming a steady cacophony. She could not bring herself to sleep. The thick muck of incessant noise began to mix with the lingering sense of adrenaline that always remained inside her after emotional trauma. She stared at the bare, white ceiling.

"I hate your trailer," she said.

"A man doesn't need a palace to get along."

"Just tell me your childhood home is better than this."

"My childhood home is better than this." He rested his head on her shoulder. They had agreed to retreat, taking both their cars, to the farmhouse until they knew what to do next.

"I don't think we should stay in the South," she said.

"What?"

"People here are just too goddamned fucking ignorant."

"People are people all over."

"I've thought about moving to Portland for years now."

"Maine?"

"Oregon."

"I see." He wiped his hand across his face and shifted upright. "I don't know what kind of welding jobs they got up there but I'd be willing to think about it. I have all my connections here though. Harold knows a guy in a custom shop."

"I know it's far away, but I think you'd like it too. There's a ton of outdoor stuff out there. They'd probably hand you another instructor's job considering the circumstances."

"What? That I got let go for punching a kid?"

"That you got fired for being with me."

They paused.

"Let's not talk about this now. It's not going to do any good," he said.

"Whatever." Sandy looked out at the kudzu. Even in the moonlight the leaves formed together like an endless expanse of blackness stretching for miles, crawling across bushes and climbing splintered telephone poles. Her heart was pounding. She could feel herself begin to shiver. She was on the threshold of yet another panic attack.

"Are you cold?" he asked.

"I'm about to have a panic attack."

"Do you need some aspirin?"

"Just hold me, please."

He wrapped his long arms around her and kissed the back of her neck. Her body began to shake in short, violent bursts.

"Tell me an Indian story."

"How about you tell me a story from your childhood."

She paused for a tremor, then said, "I got to breast feed kittens once."

"How?"

"We rescued some kittens from a storm drain and ended up feeding them. We soaked our t-shirts in baby formula and let them nurse on them."

"They didn't bite you?"

"No, of course not."

"What happened to the kittens?"

"We gave them to the Humane Society for adoption," she said. "Tell me a story from your childhood."

Yona scratched his chin and repositioned himself. "My grandmother always told me that when my mother was a child, she'd talk to raccoons."

"How do you say raccoons in Cherokee?" she asked, quivering.

"Guh-lee."

"Gully?"

"No, guh-lee," he said.

"Will raccoons approach people?"

"Thing about raccoons is they're shy when they're alone, but in numbers there isn't much they're afraid of. That includes fire and the sound of a shotgun. They can be vicious little fuckers. Anyway, so my grandma used to tell me that my ma would sit in the woods near the house at night with some bread soaked in my granddaddy's whiskey and wait for the raccoons. She'd feed'em and talk to'em and eventually the raccoons came to trust her. When they were going through our trash and making a mess all my ma had to do was ask them to go away, that her folks were sleeping, and the raccoons obliged. Now there was another critter that my grandparents liked even less than the raccoons: possums. They were these giant ugly rats hanging out on our porch and pecking at our garbage. They couldn't stand'em. My grandma said that the closest friend to the possums were the bears and wherever the possums went they were certainly going to tell the bears to follow. They were like scouts for the bears. Well, the possums were fixing to tell the bears about an Indian family with a bunch of sheep. The bears were going to eat these sheep after killing the dogs and killing the Indians. The problem was that possums didn't listen to people, so there was nothing my folks could do to persuade the possums otherwise. But my mother was friends with the raccoons who the possums got along with just fine. My mom got to be the mediator between the raccoons and the possums and saved the family and the sheep.

"After my grandma told me that story, every time I saw a raccoon I'd try and thank it and tell it who I was."

"Why didn't she name you Guh-Lee?"

"Because it's a shitty name and Yona sounds better. Almost sounds like Joseph."

"It wouldn't be a bad name," she said.

"I like my name just fine."

"Where did your mom learn all that Indian witchcraft stuff?"

"It's just part of the culture. No, in real life she was just a messed-up hippie, hanging out with the local Berdache folk."

"Berdache folks?"

"Yeah, two-spirited people. Transgender. It's been a huge part of native life for centuries."

"What do you burn 'em to the stake for a good harvest?"

"No, they had a higher place in society. It was normal. Some even said the two-spirited people had magical powers."

"I have magical powers."

"You sure do."

They lie while she shook for a few minutes longer and eventually fell asleep as her attack subsided.

CHAPTER NINE

S andy had lost sight of Yona's truck once they exited the highway and headed down a series of winding back roads. The
rainstorm continued unabated as they rolled through the
main street of a blink-and-miss hamlet known as Sharon.

Yona called her on his cell phone. "How far away from me are
you?"

"I've completely lost you, but I have the address in my GPS.
Don't worry about me."

"The roads get pretty strange up ahead. Just call me if you run
into any problems."

"I will."

"I'll see you in an hour or so."

"Okay."

She drove with complete attention on the road, the British
accent of her generic GPS system, and the ambient thump of her
techno music. She preferred driving without Yona. It was freer.

She could listen to something besides bluegrass riffs and Merle Haggard.

The tree line abruptly ended, giving way to a sea of cow pastures. She spent the next few minutes avoiding potholes on a particularly bad stretch of road. The road signs had sustained numerous volleys of buckshot, preventing most travelers from reading them. The GPS told her to turn and she entered another grouping of trees where the asphalt became smooth once again. The forested road became so dense she switched on her headlights. It was only two o'clock in the afternoon.

She parked at a small convenience store. A single gas pump accruing a flaking outer shell of rust stood in the lot. She walked inside with the intention of getting something to drink. A young boy sat behind the front desk reading a Batman comic book.

"Hello," he said without looking up.

She smiled at him. "Hello." She lingered around the drinks in the cooler, spotting an old brand she recalled from her time on Edisto Island. She held the green glass bottle of Dr. Enuf and decided to buy it.

The corkboard near the soda fountain displayed twenty missing-persons fliers. Their pictures stared back at Sandy with calm, placid faces, oddly detached from reality as if they were not entirely human. She could not connect with the blank and sometimes dubious stares of the elderly Jacob Greggs, the obviously strung-out, 23-year-old Verona Vanderborg, or the dazed, bloodshot eyes of convicted burglar Mikhail Valenzuela who purportedly suffered from epilepsy. Those were only three of the faces. The rest were children smiling in photos that had been isolated from school yearbooks and family albums. All of them had gone missing, wandering off into the dense foliage and never seen again, or cajoled into the dark van by an unseen stranger.

She walked to the front desk and set the bottle down. The boy set his comic aside and rang up her total. She gestured at the corkboard and said, "There's a lot of amber alerts running through here."

He handed gave her the change and looked at the fliers. "Yeah, I guess so."

She popped the cap on the bottle opener nailed to the wall and drifted back to the photos. No child had been missing for more than three months. She sipped the soda pop and returned to her car.

CHAPTER TEN

The road was narrow. She found herself driving slower as she passed through a creaking steel bridge. The capacity rate painted on the side was long gone after years of direct sunlight and falling rain. The structure rang out a hollow, metallic echo as Sandy cautiously tapped her shoe against the gas petal, and scooted along the planks as if she were driving through a neglected piano. The dark, slick wood slightly gave underneath the weight of her tires. She reached the other side of the rushing, distended creek and continued down the road. The Dr. Enuf kept her alert as she steered through the frequent turns, crushing dead twigs and the overgrown branches of low hanging rhododendrons.

Never in her life had she seen an area so objectively rural. Everything before her was in its own peculiar way an extension of Yona's often hermetic personality. Living out here probably made a man quiet and hard, endowed him with a wry sense of humor, and slowed his mind to a steadier pace, which allowed him to think

clearer instead of uselessly contemplating the passage of time.
There was also the possibility that she gave too much credence-
like most North Americans-to the bucolic lifestyle. Whatever the
case may have been, she was passing by much more than just trees,
seemingly derelict homes, and empty clapboard shacks. There was
something exceptionally unusual about this country. Her imagination began to fill the gaps of gray poking through the dismal, green
canopy. She could picture faces she had once seen, regurgitated
by her mind and refracted by the limitations of memory, looking
back at her through the empty windows like ghosts.

The living faces she eventually encountered were not unlike
the eerie forms she had invented. Several shirtless men and overweight women looked fixedly at her car with frowns of suspicion.
She felt herself threatened by these backwoods, country folk: the
inbred substance of legend and cinematic terror. These people actually existed.

Three miniscule figures emerged from the dewy grass on the
left side of the road. She stopped the car, allowing a precession
of grunting woodchucks pass. There was a trailer a few feet from
where she idled the vehicle. An elderly man in a plastic lawn chair
looked directly into her eyes and stood up to walk toward her car
as she waited for the rodents. When the woodchucks reached the
sweet grass, she sped away and watched the old man set his hands
in his pockets from the rearview mirror.

She followed the road up a steep incline and turned, at the cue
of the GPS, onto a gravel road only wide enough for a single car.
Thorns and crooked brambles scraped her mirrors and windows as
she drove less than 12 miles per hour. She wasn't sure how Yona's
truck could have squeezed its way through the passage and, for
the first time, she began to worry that her GPS was not accurately

calibrated. She saw a doe running parallel to the car and stopped once again to watch it run in between the tree trunks until it vanished.

She finally reached the end of the gravel and cruised up the concrete driveway leading to the wood-paneled house. The bed of Yona's truck was empty and several lights shined through the windows. She almost knew the house would have wallpaper in the kitchen, a shag carpet in the living room, wagon wheels and shotguns displayed above the fireplace, and a smell in the air that reminded her of crowded antique shops. She parked her car and walked out into the front lawn. She could see the field where the sheep once grazed and a red barn in the distance. A dense mist rolled off the foothills beyond the valley. She wandered into the field for a while, hoping to see another deer. Instead she saw a long object matting down a section of grass. At first, she assumed it was a snake and then a wayward branch. She walked closer and picked it up. The wooden shaft was smooth and dark. An enormous claw shifted through the grass as she held the wooden handle. She raised the scythe and looked at its rusted blade. The edge was still reasonably sharp.

Yona stood on the upper-level deck and called out to her. "You gonna come inside?"

"In a minute," she said. She walked out into the field and observed the mist for several minutes, before reluctantly inching her way back to the house.

CHAPTER ELEVEN

The inside of the house didn't look as old as she had expected. There was no orange shag carpet or pervasive smell of aging wood in the air, but there were framed paintings of nature scenes decorating the walls alongside an antique shotgun. She recognized one of the paintings as Sequoyah with his red turban and tobacco pipe. There was also an impressionist work of a stag racing through the woodland.

Yona had already plugged in the refrigerator and stowed the food away. She walked through the dark kitchen, noticing there were no family photographs. A small stationary set complete with linen paper, envelopes, and a book of old stamps lay in glass display case near the kitchen. There was a large bookshelf in the living room. She stepped across the carpet and opened one of the thicker, hardback editions. It was in Cherokee; strange, calligraphic symbols; some too foreign to decipher while others appeared to have been borrowed directly from English.

There was a randomly placed sink and mirror built into the wall of the narrow hallway. She touched the end of the dry bowl and felt a small crack in the enamel. In the adjacent room, Yona was spreading out the sheets to the double bed where his grandparents once slept and probably died. On top of the oaken armoire was an elaborate lace doily and ceramic chamber pot. Instead of a dream catcher, a crucifix hung from a single nail driven halfway into the wall.

"Were your grandparents catholic?"

"No, we went to a Baptist Church up the ridge here."

"Where did they buy all the paintings?"

"I had a great uncle who ran a gallery on the reservation."

"Did he paint as well?"

"No, but he played the banjo as a hobby, I believe." Yona held the sheet under his chin as he folded it.

"I'm gonna go down into the basement."

"We don't really have a basement. It's just a dirty cellar."

Sandy walked out of the room. She opened the door at the far side of the kitchen and walked down the carpeted steps to the cellar. The concrete floor was cold and abrasive. In the corner was a pile of old camping equipment, a pair of roller-skates, and a shelf of empty mason jars. There was some yarn stowed further away into the darkness. She wiped the cobwebs from the spools and rested her hand against the soft material. It was all that remained of his grandparents lives raising sheep. There was an oxidized pile of scrap metal and an old arc welder against the wall. She could imagine a teenage Yona working down here in the macabre cellar; his welding shield pulled over his face like an anonymous torturer as sparks dribbled onto the floor like drops of water. Bach's Toccata and Fugue seemed to bleed through the walls as one of the incandescent light bulbs flickered. She turned back and looked through the camping equipment, interested in discovering more about Yona's childhood. The tent and rolled sleeping bags were old and reeked of citronella and molasses. Her parents never took her camping. They went to amusement parks and carnivals, movies and restaurants. Her parents solved her problems with ice cream and swift, unaffectionate pats on the back. In many ways, Sandy envied the rural lifestyle Yona had lived. Nothing looked pretentious or unnecessary. There were no cartoons, advertisements, colorful characters promoting breakfast cereals, or McDonalds toys scattered on the front lawn. Yona grew up in a quiet, dignified environment full of free-roaming deer, indigenous languages, and trees as far as the eye could possibly see.

She removed a thin tarpaulin and found a box of red, lacquered wood. She sat down on the floor and rested the box on her knees. It was heavy. She was hoping for a chess set or a vintage bottle of whiskey. She flipped the peculiar retracting mechanism that held the box together and opened it. The hinges squeaked. She looked at the contents: a leather gun belt with plain leather holsters holding two, wood-handled, black revolvers and a switchblade. The belt buckle clinked against the top of the box as she lifted it, unfolding the holstered guns. They sagged and produced a leathery wobbling sound. She refolded the gun belt and set it back in the box. She pulled out the switchblade, flicking the end of the lever. The blade snapped out in an instant. It was sharp on both edges. She left the knife unfolded and closed the box. She figured she'd wear the holsters later on if she ever got bored.

In the opposite corner she saw the flimsy wooden door to the backyard. It was more of a hinged plank kept shut by a single latch than a door. There was a gaping hole in the lower right corner. It was big enough for any dog or raccoon to fit through. Kneeling down, she could see a muddy slope in the earth beyond the frame, suggesting that something had been sliding in and out of the musty cellar. Sandy pulled a large sheet of tarnished metal and set it against the doorway. She then moved one of the empty wooden shelves and leaned it against the wall.

"What are you doing down there?" Yona said at the edge of the stairs.

"There's a hole in the door to the yard here, I'm just covering it with a shelf." She went back up the stairs and closed the door behind her.

"It's an old house. Things are bound to be falling apart here and there," he said.

"What are the cowboy guns for?"

"Family heirloom."

"You don't have any bullets for them do you?"

"Somewhere around here, I guess."

They gathered a few more things from the back of her car and switched every light on as the day ended. They ate oven-baked pizza and drank light beer for dinner without saying much. While Yona took a shower, Sandy sat in the basement and smoked three cigarettes. She played with the guns a little and then felt a sudden overwhelming sense of anxiety. She was adrift and unsure of what to do next with her life. Not since college had she ever felt so unhappy and unsure of things. There was nothing worse than the unknown.

CHAPTER TWELVE

Yona couldn't sleep. He left Sandy in the bedroom and entered the kitchen. There was a pack of cigarettes on the counter. He opened the window as he lit one with a strike-anywhere match. He thought about listening to the relaxation tapes but remembered that he left them at his desk in the trailer. He looked at the pitch-black box in the living room, its antiquated knobs forever set to channel three. The television no longer worked. He smoked the cigarette down to the fiberglass filter, exhaling out the window, and tossed it down the sink with a brief spurt of water from the faucet. He sat down at the kitchen table and quietly folded his hands together. He could hear Sandy crawl out of bed and use the bathroom. As the toilet water flushed, she staggered into the kitchen and sat down beside him at the table. Her face looked tired but sober. She reached out and touched the balled clump of his scarred hands. His right hand unfolded and eclipsed hers.

"I had a horrible nightmare," she said.

"That happens sometimes when you're under stress. I had one awful dream after the other when I was in the hospital," he said. "What happened in your dream?"

"I found a new job working for a doctor. But he wasn't a normal doctor. He worked in a McDonald's franchise basement where he tortured people and conducted experiments. He made me open a man's chest cavity with a pair of salad forks and take out the heart with hedge clippers. He dipped infants in metal drums filled with acid. He gave the left over hunks of flesh to the fry cooks upstairs."

Yona laughed. "Jesus fucking Christ, Sandy!"

They both laughed for a bit. Something was on her mind.

"You told me a long time ago that your grandfather died of a heart attack. Was it in bed?"

"No one died in the bed you're sleeping in," he said. "He died in that hallway. My grandmother was cooking in the evening and...it all happened in a few seconds."

"Did he have heart disease?"

"We weren't sure. He wasn't an unfit man but he was old and he liked his whiskey. Drank two glasses in the living room over there every night before bed."

"What was he like when he drank?"

"Asleep," said Yona. "I wouldn't have categorized him as an alcoholic. He was a quiet, stern man most of his life. I think his upbringing made him bitter. Most Indians in his youth were unfathomably poor and a lot of them were beaten down in the Indian Schools. He worked and ate. Fixed things when they needed to be fixed. He was very proud of my interest in welding. Being a skilled worker was-at least to him-a great aspiration."

"Did he watch westerns?"

"God no, he hated westerns. It's just a bunch of white guys shootin' Indians."

"How did your grandma die?"

"Peacefully. She was sitting on the porch in her rocking chair, wrapped in a shawl."

"What did you know about your late mother?"

"Nothing I haven't already told you." He gave her a weary, sleep-deprived smile and wiped his face.

She thought for a few moments and asked another question to postpone what was actually troubling her.

"Why do you think Mr. Rice shot his wife and then himself?"

"The same reason stock brokers jump from office buildings. He buried himself alive with debt, a loveless marriage, wife probably killed his dog. He was probably a little crazy to begin with. Everything just came full circle. At the same time though, anyone's capable of anything. I think he just made a bizarre decision. I don't think too far into it after that or else I get depressed."

"Yeah." She paused. Her legs fidgeted up and down with anticipation and stomach-churning fear.

"I'm scared," she said.

"So am I."

"I don't want this place to become limbo for us while we don't know what to do with ourselves."

"Catastrophe always leads to opportunity."

"Is that Cherokee wisdom?"

"Chinese proverb. A minister would say 'God never shuts one door without opening another.'"

She sighed.

"We can do anything right now. If you want to go to Portland, Oregon, let's do it. There's no better time than now. Let's relax a little bit and then take the next few days to get everything planned out."

"Where did the sudden change of heart come from?"

"I've been mulling it over today and I figured, what the hell."

"There's gotta be more to it than that."

"Truth is, I've wanted to see the rest of the world since I was kid. That's what I thought welding would do for me. I wanted to work on the Alaska pipelines," he said. "I'm not afraid of taking a risk, Sandy. There's nothing ludicrous about moving to a different city, anyway. You wanna try Portland. Okay, fuck it. Let's go to Portland. Let's head out west where all the other spurn folks go to reinvent themselves. We can always come back if it doesn't work out. It's not like we have anything to lose."

"Are you serious?"

"It depends."

"On what?"

"Do you want me to go with you? I mean, do you just feel guilty that I lost my job too or do you really want me?"

She went silent. She wanted to speak but she could only stutter. Eventually she asked, "Do you want me?"

"You have to answer my question first," he asserted.

She nodded. "Please, stay with me. I need you."

He grabbed her and wrapped his hands around her shoulders. She buried her face into his shirt.

CHAPTER THIRTEEN

She woke up alone and kicked the white sheets off the bed. She could hear Yona cooking pancakes in the kitchen. Her suitcase lay on the carpet near the master bathroom door. She searched through the front flap and pulled out her medical bag. She walked into the bathroom and shut the door. The zipper made a faint swiping noise as she opened the bag filled with her supplies. The cap to the hypodermic needle twisted off and she plunged it into the brown-glass vile, filling the syringe to the line she had highlighted with permanent marker. She set the cap back on the needle and lay it on the porcelain beside the sink. There were still a few alcohol swabs at the bottom of the medical bag, which she tore open with her teeth to clean her hairless thigh. After that she switched to a fresh needle with the grace of a paramedic, tapped the syringe, squeezed the plunger to make sure liquid was coming out, and hesitated before jamming the needle into her thigh. It was customary to pull back to make sure she didn't see any blood mixing with the estrogen. She injected slowly to cut down on the pain. As she raised the needle out of her skin, a spurt of red shot out from the puncture.

"Holy shit," she said out loud.

The droplets peppered the white toilet seat and tile floor. A single dot seeped into the roll of toilet paper. It had never happened to her before. She massaged her thigh and inspected the pinprick where the needle had been. It wasn't bleeding any longer and she assumed she had hit a vein by accident. Eventually, she set her things back inside the bag and cautiously stepped out of the bathroom.

CHAPTER FOURTEEN

Half of the sky went dark gray as a storm approached from the east. They drove into town, passing more fields of kudzu and shrubs. Sandy had her window down so the sound of the rushing air would silence the Merle Haggard album in the CD player. The scent of copper lingered in the air.

"Can't you buy an iPod?"

"It's not like I can have headphones on when I'm driving."

She watched the foliage vanish past her as the truck rolled along the road. There was a young boy standing idly in the kudzu wearing nothing but brown overalls. He sneered at Sandy with a raised upper lip.

"These hillbillies are a trip."

"What do you mean?"

"I didn't think anyone actually lived like this."

"Out in the woods?"

"In cabins and trailers out in the woods."

"Oh yeah, there's hill folk," he said, smiling.

They parked in the gravel lot behind a thrift store and walked along the sidewalk of Brevard. Light rainfall began to darken the concrete and cobbled brick. They walked past antique shops and ice cream parlors. There was a tourist bureau and a pottery store. In spite of the rain, several people were still passing the storefronts and crossing the streets with the unmistakable signs of leisure in hand: popsicles, colored maps, and digital cameras.

"This is a tourist town," she said.

"What did you think it was going to be?"

"Not this."

As the rain increased, they walked into a Southern café and took seats next to the window. The waitress was pregnant. Sandy read her nametag. Her name was Jezebel.

"That's a beautiful name," she said.

The waitress smiled, "Thank you. What can I get y'all to drink?"

"A root beer."

"Can I have water with lemon?" asked Yona.

"Of course." She wrote down their drink orders and smiled again before disappearing behind the lunch counter.

"What did you dream about last night?" she asked him.

"I don't remember."

"You're no fun."

"No, I honestly don't remember what I dreamt."

"You're not introspective enough."

"Maybe not."

The waitress eventually came with their drinks and took their order. Yona asked for a Reuben and Sandy, the fried green tomatoes. Jezebel walked away cheerfully.

Sandy drummed her fingers against the tablecloth and stared

out the window in a trance of deep thought, mulling over the possibilities of a new life in Oregon. Yona stared at her, wondering what she was thinking.

A teenage couple walked into the dining room of the café and sat down in the table parallel to Sandy and Yona. They both looked pale and sullen. Their clothes were dark and studded with metal spikes. The girl's hair was dyed black with light-brown roots rising up from her scalp. Sandy watched them as they gave their drink orders to Jezebel without looking at her, staring at the laminated menus.

"I used to be a rude little bitch like that," she whispered.

"Don't stare at them."

She turned back to Yona. "Have you ever been arrested?"

"You mean as a teenager?"

"Yeah."

"Nope. Have you?"

"I was at a party that got busted and I jumped out the kitchen window. An officer chased me into the golf course and then gave up. Everyone got tickets except me."

"I think I remember this story."

A different waitress brought their food and they ate in silence. The bell jingled as the door opened and a man with a white canvas duffle bag and denim clothing entered the café. He screamed at the top of his lungs, startling each patron as they immediately turned to see him.

"This country here is plagued by a disease!"

Jezebel ran past the lunch counter. "We have a no soliciting sign on our door."

"I'm not selling anything. The woods surrounding us...they're all over. They come from the west to preach their word. They're all around us."

Jezebel pointed to the waitress behind the counter. "Call the police."

"The police can't save you from their word. It's a cruel, vile word. Unholy in every way. The police are in their pocket. It's the children. They're inhuman. Vile, satanic children ready to kill anyone. They'll find your children and they'll kill'em."

The teenagers next to Sandy began to clap sarcastically.

"Nothing's funny about what's coming. I've seen them and their word."

As the other waitress picked up the phone, the man immediately ran out after throwing a pile of pamphlets on the ground from the canvas bag. Jezebel picked them up and tossed them in the wastebasket.

"I apologize," she said. "It happens now and then."

They walked outside under the covered half of the sidewalk as the rain fell. Yona pulled out two cigarettes from the pack.

"If we're going to start a new life, we should quit," she said.

Yona nodded as he lit the cigarettes and puffed smoke.

"We're too old to smoke," she said. "It's not high school anymore."

"Too old to smoke and too young to die."

She flicked her cigarette at him with a sarcastic grin spreading across her face.

"Hey, I paid for that."

"Money comes and goes," she said.

He pulled on the filter. She could hear the tobacco crackle.

"Did your parents smoke?"

"You mean my grandparents?"

"Yeah. Sorry, I got confused."

"My grandpa had a pipe he'd puff on from time to time, but I never saw Mabel do anything."

"Your grandmother's name was Mabel?"

"I didn't already tell you?"

"No, I don't think I ever asked."

"My grandmother's name was Mabel Bridger and my grandpa was Cain Bridger."

"Beautiful names," she said. "What was your mother's name?"

He hesitated for a moment. "Ama."

"Anna?"

"No, Ama," he said. "It's the Cherokee word for water."

"Why did they name her that?"

"That's how she was born into this world, through water." Yona held the cigarette in his lips and reached his hand outward to catch a few droplets.

The road was littered with fallen twigs and a thin layer of sediment. Sandy had won command of the radio and they were listening to the local station's news program.

Yona spread his hand across his stomach. "I don't think the corned beef in that Rueben was cooked properly."

"You just have a sensitive stomach," she said. "It's probably the vinegar in the sauerkraut."

"I have a cast-iron stomach. I swallowed chewing tobacco once and held it down."

"That's impossible."

"I've done it. I was on a tour bus with-"

Sandy stopped him and turned up the volume on the radio. "I wanna listen to this real quick."

The radio newscaster did her best to hide her drawl, speaking in a soft, monotone voice. "The Transylvania County Sheriff's Department confirmed yesterday that the body of twelve-year-old Benjamin Nichols was found by the North Carolina Park Service and later identified by Nichols' aunt and uncle, his legal guardians. Nichols had been missing for two weeks when a hiker notified the park service of a body near Haverbrook Mountain creek. He was last seen playing in his aunt and uncle's backyard when he allegedly wandered off into the woods beyond their residence. Nichols was diagnosed at the age of four with autism. The Deputy Coroner released a statement saying that Nichols had drowned. His death was mostly likely a tragic accident, according to Sheriff Frank Emanuel."

Yona cringed. "Poor guy."

"I think I saw his picture in the gas station," she said.

"The gas station?"

"I stopped at a little gas station on my way up here. They had a display of missing persons."

"That's the way things work out here being so close to the woods and all."

"Nobody drowns in a creek."

"Well, the kid was autistic."

"That doesn't mean he was retarded."

Yona's eyes briefly scanned the periphery of the rearview mirror. There was a sudden flash of potent red and blue light. He thought he saw an ambulance when the siren sounded off twice. He gathered his thoughts and realized there was a police cruiser behind them. He drove into the grass on the side of the road and shut down the engine.

"Speak of the devil." Sandy sighed and turned off the radio. "What do you think we've done?"

"Might've been going too fast or maybe that new light finally busted. Nothing to worry about."

They waited for a few breathless moments. Yona kept his hands on the wheel.

The officer stepped out of the cruiser and pulled up his brown pants. He slammed the door and walked over to the truck. They could hear his boots crunch and scuffle against the dirty asphalt. Yona rolled down his window as the police officer rested one hand on the roof and the other on the butt of his pistol. His wrinkled, pockmarked skin made him look old but the hair under his hat was still full and jet-black. His face was so well-shaven Sandy wondered if he could even grow a beard. Yona's face was just as smooth. She had always been curious about men who were able to shave without cutting themselves as their skin became looser throughout the years.

The officer didn't speak. He just looked at them. It wasn't an austere or admonishing look, but a dubious, almost blank expression.

"Is there anything wrong?" Yona asked.

The officer cleared his throat. "License an' reg'stration, please."

Yona bent over Sandy's lap to open the glove compartment, taking out the paperwork. He fished out his leather wallet where he kept his license and handed everything to the cop who inspected the license first.

"South Carolina?"

"Yes sir."

"Thought so on account of your plate. My wife's from

Timmonsville."

"Can't say I've heard of it," said Yona.

"It's a small town." The officer had a subdued way of talking. Sandy leaned her head closer to the window just to hear him. She thought his soft voice would have been inviting in different circumstances. He handed the license back and began reading the registration.

"We're just staying here for a couple of days," said Sandy.

He cleared his throat again and handed the registration back to Yona. An SUV was coming down the opposite side of the road at a steady pace. The officer's attention was abruptly diverted to a box turtle standing in the oncoming vehicle's path.

"If ya'll could hang on fer one second." He raised his index finger to demonstrate the amount of time.

Yona put the paper back in the glove compartment and looked at Sandy with one eyebrow raised. "What the hell is this guy doing?"

"Just be patient and play the game," she said.

"Is he even playing a game?"

They watched as he halted the SUV with one hand. He knelt down and picked up the turtle by its shell. It scuttled away into the dewy grass as he released it on the other side. The driver of the SUV rolled down his own window and spoke to the officer. Yona and Sandy couldn't hear anything. The officer eventually slapped the side of the hulking vehicle in a playful manner and the driver took off. As he made his way back to the truck, he unwrapped and ate a small chocolate coin from his pocket.

"Sorry, 'bout that. He's a friend."

"Were we driving too fast?" asked Yona.

Sandy read his nametag. His surname was Thatcher.

"No, you wadn't goin' too fast. But you were swerving. Have you had any drinks today?"

"No sir."

"I didn't figure. I'as smelling your breath the whole time now." He patted Yona on the shoulder. "Just keep them eyes on the road, son."

Yona smiled in relief. "Of course, officer."

"Was she talking to you?" Thatcher smiled.

"We were listening to the radio."

He laughed. "Yeah, that'd do it. Where y'all from in South Carolina?"

"Greenville."

"What brings you up here?"

They paused.

Sandy said, "We're moving to Oregon."

"Shoot, that's a ways off. You folks e'er been out West?"

"Not yet."

"It's quite something," he said. "Y'all got family out there?"

"No."

Thatcher stopped to cough and look at the sky. He frowned. "It's fixin' to rain again. Y'all drive safe. I'm sorry if I took too much of your time. Good luck in Oregon."

"Thank you."

Officer Thatcher walked away and stepped back into the cruiser. Yona watched him drive past them before steering back onto the road. "Did you think I was swerving?" he asked Sandy.

"No, you seemed to be going pretty straight to me. You did have your hand on your stomach though."

"I don't know. He was taking his sweet time. We were definitely being checked out."

"How come?"

"Just being a nosy cop I guess."

CHAPTER FIFTEEN

She once asked him about his leg, why he had a partial limp in his stride. Yona massaged his shin as he spoke, telling her about the red steel beam. Somehow it had waddled off the crane's hook, falling twenty feet. There was no time to think. He was drinking a grape soda and looking at his boots when he saw the approaching shadow on the concrete and impulsively dove forward, extending his body horizontally. If he had just stepped a single foot to the right, the beam would have only smacked the concrete and rebounded.

He didn't remember screaming or the beam being lifted off his leg. He didn't recall the faces of the paramedics or the ride to the hospital.

The settlement was generous and helped pay for his surgery and physical therapy. On Mondays and Wednesdays he met with a short blonde woman named Trisha in a brightly colored room where he learned how to walk again.

He used a cane for eight months after his therapy regimen and fell into a profound depression. He sat on his couch in the evening and got drunk off cheap lager and filled his ashtray with one cigarette after another. He felt like a coward for not returning to construction and wondered if any of his old friends had lost respect for him.

Eventually, he found another job and was able to discard the cane, slowly regaining his self-confidence as he tested to become a welding instructor.

He didn't like it when colleagues talked about their injuries waking them up or giving them a sense of mortality. His accident left everything murky and unclear. Even the death of his grandparents and the shattered tungsten rod had not altered the manner in which he thought. Nothing felt real. He still took life for granted. Colors were not as vibrant, jokes he had once loved seemed puerile, and sex and masturbation became perfunctory. He was not the same person. His humor became cynical and his tolerance for violence and tragedy, whether at the movies or on the news, was unprecedented. A membrane of numbness surrounded him that very few things were able to penetrate. Sandy was one of the few.

CHAPTER SIXTEEN

They sat on the wood balcony with a pitcher of lemonade between them, watching the pink sun lower on the far side of the mountain range. Yona stretched his bare feet over the floor planks. His calluses were too tough for the splinters. Sandy shuffled the ice in her perspiring glass and took a sip of the weak mixture.

"In a minute the sky'll turn blue, just before it goes all black," he said.

"I prefer purple sunsets."

A short gust of wind shook a few twigs loose from the oak and they fell against the roof. The sky overhead was already turning a dim blue that intensified the colors of the tree line.

"I bet it was something to have the sheep out around this time."

"How come?"

"The color of their wool must have been beautiful."

"Nothing particularly special about it," he said. "Sheep were sheep."

Sandy drank more lemonade and caressed her feet against the gnarled wood. "What are you gonna do about your trailer?" she asked.

"I own the damn thing. I'm just gonna let it sit. Ain't nothing I need."

"Isn't that illegal?"

"I guess. Just let the city take care of it. They'll probably burn it before it gets too run down anyway."

"Why'd you move into a trailer in the first place?"

"I lived in a nice apartment when I moved up to Asheville, but the job I had at the college wasn't so high paying. Plus, I was prepping to get my instructor's license. I ended up tapping into my reserve, my settlement money I mean, to pay the rent. When I came back to Greenville, I didn't want to spend too long in the motels, so I put up the money for a trailer. I figured I didn't want to deal with rent anymore. Thought I'd save up too, get a house one day." He raised his glass and drank. "Yep, Palm Tech wasn't a bad job."

"Let's not talk about Palmetto Tech anymore," she said.

Yona dug out the grime under his fingernail with his teeth, spitting it to the side like a sunflower seed, and drank another gulp of lemonade.

"Two miles out, past that ridge there, is the fire brigade dispatch tower." He pointed using his glass.

"Is it still in use?"

"Sure, the park service always used it. There hasn't been a forest fire here in a long time." He thought for a moment. "That's right across from Haverbrook creek."

"Yeah?"

He clarified. "That's where they found the kid, the one who

drowned."

"Oh, from the radio," she said. "I remember. How do you know that?"

"I had to walk out to the tower when my mom cut herself with the kitchen knife."

"You didn't have a telephone?"

"No telephone."

"That's ridiculous."

"We couldn't get connected back then and my folks weren't gonna pay to have a dispatch system installed just to call the ranger station."

"So you walked out into the woods to use their phone?"

"Normally we could just walk up the street and use the pay phone or the store manager's phone to call someone if we needed to."

"Did you have to walk eight miles in the snow to use the outhouse or pump clean drinking water?"

"Very funny."

"Didn't you ever get lonely when you were a kid?" she asked. "It never got difficult being so isolated here?"

"No, there were plenty of other kids at school. There were one or two other Cherokee kids actually. I don't remember if they spoke any, but we hung out. We wanted to play cops and robbers all the time so the other kids wouldn't play cowboys and Indians, because they'd always make us the Indians."

"I don't mean like at school. I just mean, didn't it get strange for your folks having to live so alone?"

"They were the types of people who were alright with that," he said.

The sun eventually sunk beneath the earth, its glow doused by twilight. The trees rustled in the calm winds, and soon the vista before them disappeared into an opaque void without color or depth. Sandy could barely see the edge of the balcony outlined against the night. She carefully poured another glass of lemonade.

"I have to pee," said Yona. He walked inside.

Sandy looked up and could see the stars better than ever. She never went to summer camp or took long trips with the family. Stars of such brilliance only existed on planetarium walls during second grade field trips. She listened to an owl in the distance and the crack of a falling branch, unable to tell how far off in the distance they were.

Yona walked back onto the balcony.

"My god, that's beautiful," she said, looking directly upward.

"Isn't it?"

"It's just so dark out here. It didn't scare you when you were a kid?"

"No, it never did. I got scared when I heard animal noises but I was never afraid of the dark," he said. "I actually liked it. I always thought darkness was like a blanket that covered everything when I was real young."

"What do you mean?"

"My grandmother would sit me on her lap and she'd point out to the forest. By nightfall, every tree and thicket looked like this big ol' mass of just black, empty space," he said. "When it was dark, I didn't think that the shapes and shadows I saw were the same thing as the trees and fields. I thought it was a sort of substance or cloud-like thing that covered the woods at night. I called it 'tree black.' My grandma would point and say, 'What's that out there?' and I'd say, 'Tree black, covering the woods.' I wasn't sure what would happen to me if I walked out into it. I used to have dreams that it was sticky and it would stick to a person forever like tar. I thought that's where ghosts came from. They were people who walked out into the 'tree black' and they would rummage through peoples' homes looking for some way to scrape it off their skin."

"How do you remember all this stuff from your childhood?"

"I guess I just do."

"I can't remember anything. My self-awareness began in middle school."

Yona smiled in the darkness. "You didn't wear dresses when you were a kid?"

"Not until high school did I work up the courage to wear a skirt. It was a friend's house party. I dressed up as a Goth girl and nobody knew who I was." She thought for a moment as she sipped her lemonade and was struck by an old memory. "I do remember crying when my parents wouldn't let me be Cinderella for Halloween."

Yona chuckled.

"I was devastated. My sister got to be one of the girls from Sailor Moon. I was so jealous."

"I don't remember celebrating Halloween. We celebrated Christmas and Easter but that was about it."

"What about at school?"

"No," he said. "Most of the kids had the same situation as I did. We lived in a rural area. You just couldn't go trick-or-treating."

"The Day of the Dead was awesome in Mexico."

"Don't they celebrate that in November?"

"It's the first couple days of November. Even if you're not in Mexico City, the parades and festivals are beautiful."

They finished off the lemonade and sat in darkness.

"You wanna go to bed?" he asked.

"Yeah, I'm getting tired."

He lifted the empty pitcher and opened the glass door, locking it behind them.

Yona brushed his teeth over the hallway's built-in sink while Sandy used the master bathroom toilet. She also brushed her teeth, holding the toothbrush in the side of her mouth like a cigar as she wiped. She was never a huge fan of multi-tasking but she had learned not to waste time in the bathroom during her college years. She looked at her feet on the tile. Her maroon nail polish was cracked. She wanted to paint them a different color, something lighter to signal a new beginning.

Yona called from the hallway. "We should go to the grocery store tomorrow."

"Is it in town?"

"No, there's a little place up the road last time I checked."

"Okay." She sprayed green froth from her mouth as she spoke. She stood up and pulled her gray panties to her hips and flushed the toilet. Yona walked into the bathroom and spat in the sink.

"You think you ever wanna go hiking while we're up here?" he asked.

"We should probably get some bug spray."

"There's not a lot of insects up here in the mountains. That's in the low country area."

"Yeah, but there's still mosquitoes."

"There's not too many of them."

"I don't care. I don't like mosquito bites."

She wiped her face with a towel and swigged from a bottle of Listerine. Yona did the same and grabbed onto her breasts. She gave him a dead stare. He grinned. They spat the blue liquid into the sink at the same time.

She walked into the dark bedroom and pushed the covers back. Yona climbed on top of her and gave her a kiss. She latched onto his wide shoulders and let him shift her to the right side of the bed before kissing her neck.

Intimacy was not complicated. Sex was complicated. They were limited when it came to sex. Sandy still had a penis and didn't see herself putting up the several thousand dollars it would cost to remove it anytime soon. Yona didn't expect her to have it removed, but he wasn't sure how he felt either. She wondered if he pretended that it wasn't there, erect and in his face, when they first began to have sex. As time went on their sex became less of an obstacle and they were able to enjoy themselves. Sandy asked him if he ever felt gay because of her genitals and Yona admitted to still worrying about it sometimes. He came from a working-class background. All of his friends and instructors were white Southern Baptists, and he breathed in a mild ignorance from the atmosphere. His parents were not as staunch as the white majority, but they lived and thought in simple terms as well. He had read stories in their books, however, about the two-spirited members of the old tribes: men who dressed as women and typically assumed the role of a healer, so the idea of Sandy's gender ambiguity wasn't inordinately bizarre to him. What scared him was not her biology but his own actions behind the closed bedroom doors. He was not averse to reciprocating oral sex when Sandy gave it to him first. He actually enjoyed feeling her inside his mouth, her hands running through his hair. It was afterwards when he lay in bed next to her that he couldn't help but feel awkward and somewhat perverse. She had once masturbated both their penises while he rested his head on her shoulders. That had been nice. It was the anal sex he absolutely couldn't handle. He didn't want to think of himself as a typical male willing to give and unwilling to receive, but he couldn't stand being anally penetrated. He didn't tell her his exact choice of words, but, in his mind, sodomy was disgusting and made him feel 'faggy.'

He nibbled on her breast for a short period of time. She turned to him with half her face in the pillow. He could see half of a familiar expression.

"I'm..."

"Not in the mood." He said it for her. "Got'cha."

She turned around and looked at the dark hallway. "Do you seriously want to go hiking tomorrow?" she asked.

"We don't have to."

"No, I think it sounds kinda fun."

He wrapped his arm around her. "Yeah, okay. I think we have some backpacks 'round here somewhere."

There was a sudden crash from the kitchen. She shook and sat up instantly, letting the burst of adrenaline diffuse. Yona seemed unshaken and slowly rose from the bed.

"What was that?"

"That was probably a raccoon," he said. "I'll go check it out."

He left the room. Sandy waited, gripping her chest as if to stop her heart. Yona casually walked back into the bedroom.

"Cookie jar fell off the counter."

CHAPTER SEVENTEEN

She woke up in the darkness and felt a sharp pain in her hand. Yona's elbow had been crushing it for the past few hours while she slept. He was breathing heavily like a tranquilized animal fighting off the effects of a blowgun dart. She freed her hand and massaged it. The bedroom was completely silent except for his labored, wispy breaths. She sat up and stared at a shape beyond the window she could only assume was a mass of tree branches. Her hand ached. She extended her fingers and stood up to walk into the bathroom. She stood there idly, her feet on the cold tile, waiting for her eyes to adjust before popping a few Tylenol capsules. The bathtub faucet dripped a single bead of water. She reentered the dark bedroom and lay awake beside Yona as he began to snore.

She remembered waking up in the small villa in southern Oaxaca where the tour guides slept. She would open her eyes and wipe the sweat off her brow, gazing upward at the adobe ceiling. A young boy named Ramón would knock on the door, acting as her personal alarm clock. She would open the door and rub her eyes as he told her it was almost eight o'clock and breakfast was being prepared for the tourists. He said it the same way each day as if he had practiced everything down to the high-pitched cadence in his voice. Sandy always noticed the thin scar on the left side of his face. She pulled out an American dollar or a 20-peso note and set it in his hand. He thanked her and stuffed it into his pocket. Together they walked across the sunny parking lot into the guest house, discussing what Ramón would do for a living as an adult. He wanted to move to Brazil and mine for gold.

"No, there's better things to do than that," she'd say.

"But Portuguese is so much easier than English."

"English isn't hard."

They would walk into the kitchen of the guest house where Flora was cooking eggs. She would immediately have them squeezing fresh orange juice and taking the cans of Coca-Cola out of the refrigerator to arrange them in a basket.

Sandy reemerged from her thoughts as Yona's snore intensified. She stood back up and walked down the dark hallway into the living room. The couch looked comfortable and warm. She crept down, hugging her knees, and nestled into the warped cushions. There was an elaborate blanket, which she pulled over her body to stay relatively warm. For ten minutes she drifted between thoughts until they evolved into lucid dreams.

She awoke suddenly, her eyes flashing open in a panicked instant. She was confused and looked around the room as if the problem stood before her. A distant yet shrill scream carried through the house. Sandy froze until she heard the scream once again and ran into the bedroom, fighting to maintain her balance. Yona woke up and tightly grabbed her shoulders.

"What the hell are you doing?"

"Someone's screaming outside."

"Are you serious?"

She was pulling her jeans on and tightening the belt. "Yes, I'm serious!"

"You're sure it wasn't an animal?"

"Get your fuckin' clothes on and come to the patio."

Yona stood up and slowly put his pants on. "Just calm down. We're gonna check this out."

They walked into the kitchen where he found a large flashlight under the sink and pulled an unloaded shotgun from the wall.

"Do you have any shells for that?"

He rolled his eyes at her. "Don't be ridiculous."

They stepped onto the porch as a strangely muggy breeze rustled a few twigs loose from the canopy. Yona shined the enormous bulb of the flashlight into the field. Weeds and patches of tall grass swayed in the wind. He moved the light into the trees where the tree bark went from black to varying shades tarnished pinchbeck.

"I don't see anything." He sighed. "You're absolutely sure you heard a scream?"

"It was further off into the field."

He shined the flashlight into the distance but the glare had a short range. The blood drained from his face as they heard another desperate scream.

"Oh, shit. That's coming from the shed."

"We have to call the police."

"And wait six hours for them to come out here? No, you wait here."

"Yona, no."

"I have a gun."

"It's not loaded."

"Only I know that," he said as he shifted the flashlight in his hands.

"Don't do this."

"We have to. Just wait here."

"God-fucking-damn it!" She pounded her fist against the sliding glass door.

He abandoned her, heading down the stairs. She watched as the yellow glow of the flashlight disappeared into the field.

She was alone.

The wind carried stray leaves across the green terrain and forced random creaks from the old wood of the deck, punctuating the long silences. She stood quivering in the wake of total darkness. Her knees ached as she found it more and more difficult to stand in her dirty blue jeans growing cold in the fluctuating, late-spring temperature. The splintered wood scraped the top of her bare feet. She pictured Yona's body under the shine of the nearly full moon, lying in the grass after an unimaginable calamity. She smacked the side of her temple to expel the image from her mind. The distant sound of a night bird fluttered across the tree line. She fell to her knees. A panic attack was brewing from deep within her. She strained to suppress it, to disassociate herself. Her stomach tightened as she began to breathe in short, measured intervals. The fluorescent kitchen light keeping the patio visible seemed to dim. Her heart fluttered. She stood back up and sat in the rocking chair. The night became colder as the wind increased.

"Yona!" she called out. "Yona, are you alright?"

An echoed yell responded. "Yes."

"What's going on?"

There was no answer.

A strain came over her. She dug her nails in the arm of the rocking chair. Her muscles clung to her bones like roots crumbing stone. A cramp spread from her leg to her calve muscle. Paralyzing anticipation deadened the air around the home as she kept on trying to breathe calmly. She moved the leg to offset the cramp and massaged it with the balls of her thumbs.

The yellow orb of light returned in the distance of the field. Her heart kept pounding as Yona hastily trekked back to the house. He held the flashlight with his right hand and kept the shotgun under his left. His arms wrapped around a short woman wearing a loose-fitting blue dress. Her hair was red like Sandy's but it appeared brighter and jet-black around the roots suggesting it had been dyed. It seemed to be cut at an odd angle until Sandy realized-once she was close enough-that part of her frizzy hair had been pulled out. The entire left side of the woman's scalp was bleeding onto her face, neck, and shoulders. Sandy gasped as she saw the woman was completely covered in blood not only from her head but also from enormous slashes across her calves and arms. Yona ushered the frantic woman, who had suddenly fallen silent, to the stairs of the patio.

"Get her inside," he said.

Sandy feebly opened the sliding door and helped Yona place the woman on the couch. The woman sat there with her hands folded over her lap, shivering.

"We'll call the police and an ambulance." She said it more to confirm to herself what she was about to do, as though it would make everything easier to overcome and put behind her. Sandy took her cell phone off the kitchen counter and dialed 9-1-1. She waited for a few moments with the receiver to her ear, waiting for the emergency operator. Her phone was silent. The message on the home screen read: searching for signal.

"Damn it!"

Yona sat on the coffee table across from the woman. He spoke to Sandy without taking his eyes off the blood slowly spreading into the gray fabric of the couch.

"Can you not get a signal?"

"No," she said, waving the phone above her head in false hope. "What the hell is happening outside?"

"Nothing, I just found her lying on her back near the shed." He stood up. "Come with me over here real quick."

"What?"

The woman was watching them intently and balling her dress up around her crotch as if she were hiding something valuable.

Yona whispered in Sandy's ear. This gesture frightened the woman and she began to shake even more.

"Stop panicking. You're scaring her. I need to tell you something in confidence." He turned to the woman. "We're going to go into the bathroom to get you some alcohol for your cuts okay. Then we're going to get you to an ambulance. Do you understand?"

She nodded.

They walked into the bathroom. Yona pulled out a roll of gauze, cotton balls, and bottle of rubbing alcohol from the cabinet. Sandy continued her four-count breathing exercises.

"What is it...you need...to tell me?"

Yona rifled through the cabinet until he found a nearly empty tube of Neosporin. "Something's wrong with her vagina."

"What?"

"I found her lying in the grass by the shed. She's bleeding profusely from her...you know? She's keeping her hands around it."

"And?"

"It took a lot to get her to come to the house with me. She's afraid of me. A man has done this to her. I want you to make her feel safe enough to where you can check her out."

"Let the paramedics take care of it."

"It's going to take too long, Sandy. I'm going to run up to the payphone at the shop, assuming it's still there. We have to help her ourselves. I'm going to let her watch me leave out the door and you have to calm her down and clean her cuts till I get back."

Sandy swallowed. "Alright."

They walked out of the bathroom and reentered the living room. The woman was still watching them as if they were plotting against her.

"I'm going to run down the road to call for an ambulance. I'll be back shortly."

Sandy spread the medical supplies on the coffee table and sat down next to them. She noticed for the first time that the woman was gripping her pelvic area. Blood was seeping from the couch to the carpet.

Yona ran out the door and left them.

She turned to the woman and did her best to smile. "My name is Sandy. What's yours?"

"E...liz..." She stuttered with her thick, mountain accent. "Elizabeth."

"Well, Elizabeth you're cut very badly and I need to clean your wounds."

She nodded.

"Does that mean I can help?"

"Be quick," she faintly whispered, aggression in her voice.

In complete silence they swabbed the slashes on her arms and legs with the Neosporin cream and the stinging alcohol. Sandy couldn't bear touching the deep lacerations. There were a few she could stick her fingers inside. She closed her eyes as she ran her hands along the woman's skin. It felt rough and jagged after most of the blood had congealed into a layer of crust that covered almost all of her body. Elizabeth gave short gasps when adding alcohol to her cuts. She started mumbling as Sandy wrapped her arms and legs in thick sleeves of gauze.

"I ne'er saw'em coming. It wadn't like I knew..." She trailed off into a series of muted whimpers.

As soon as they were finished, she returned to clutching her crotch.

Sandy stared at the floor and tapped her fingertips together. Her stomach churned with fear. "You're going to be okay," she said. "We're going to get an ambulance up here for you."

"And they'as gonna stick me with pinpricks and needles. I've been stuck enough."

"They're gonna make sure everything's fine."

Elizabeth fell silent.

"Elizabeth, can I ask you a serious question?"

She didn't answer.

"Elizabeth, it's important for your safety. I want to help you."

She gripped her dress tighter and began to cry.

"Elizabeth." She was relying too much on using her name. "Is there anything wrong with you...down there?"

Down there. She sounded like an eight-year-old again, too afraid to use the terminology. Sandy placed her hand on Elizabeth's gauzed leg and tried to look as harmless as possible.

"Please, let me just see what's happened. I promise I won't do anything that's going to hurt."

Sandy had never played the role of doctor. She had never fallen from a tree or broken an arm while riding her bike. Her sister hadn't been seriously hurt in her lifetime either. For the most part, Sandy had bypassed the after-hours world of long stays in the ICU and anxious clinic visits.

She doubted her ability to comfort this battered and maimed woman, bleeding on the sofa. There was not enough alcohol in the world to help her to muster the courage to lift her dress and witness what she had been hiding. A slew of brutal images raced through her mind and she began to feel nauseated. Despite all of her fear and aversion, her body was inclined to continue. She was still sitting there, doing exactly what Yona wanted.

Her hand remained on the woman's gauzed leg. "Please Elizabeth," she said. "I'm a woman too." It pained her to say that. It felt like a lie.

"You a nurse?"

"No, but I promise I won't touch or hurt you."

Elizabeth shuddered and slowly closed her eyes. She turned her head to the left and began pulling up her dress.

Sandy's face went pale. She covered her mouth with her hand.

The opposing walls of Elizabeth's labia had been evenly punctured to facilitate a thick wire, which tied the vagina shut.

Sandy nearly screamed before asking her to close her skirt.

She let her blue dress fall over her legs.

"I'm so sorry that happened to you."

Elizabeth said nothing.

"Do you need a glass of water?"

She nodded.

Sandy stood up and walked into the kitchen and poured a shallow glass of water, setting three ice cubes into the glass.

Elizabeth took the glass with both hands. She sucked on the

water through the corner of her mouth and set the drink on the coffee table next to Sandy.

A branch fell on the deck beyond the sliding door. Both women jolted in fear.

"It was just a branch."

Elizabeth had shut down. She wouldn't speak any longer.

Sandy hid her face within her hands. She could not imagine an individual sick enough to sew a woman's vagina closed. She thought about how much Elizabeth must have screamed if she was conscious when it was done. She wondered if they tied her to a bed or belted her to a cold table. She thought about the trailer trash living in the area, wondering what kind of boredom fostered such a twisted imagination. It was difficult not think of it as a misogynist's statement or religious fanatic's grand gesture of cruelty. There couldn't have been a practical purpose behind doing such a thing, unless she was pregnant. If she was, Elizabeth must have found out a few days ago. Her thin, emaciated frame didn't look big enough for her own stomach let alone an impending embryo. The stitching was most likely symbolic. Sandy could think of no better symbol of control over the female form. Tears were pulling mascara down her cheeks, mascara she didn't even remember applying.

"You're going to be okay," she said. She kept on repeating it.

CHAPTER EIGHTEEN

Yona ran up the empty, lightless road. His heavy footfalls culminated into a distressing, minimal rhythm like an old grandfather clock or a metronome: a constant reminder that time was scarce. He didn't remember the road up to the general store being as dark as it was, and he realized that he had either walked there in the day or driven during nightfall. He felt like a fool for not taking a vehicle but he was too far along now to head back. Breathing became difficult. He hadn't run this much since high school. Right now would be the worst possible time to have a sudden heart attack, he thought, wondering if his smoking and affinity for lager would set him down the same path as his grandfather. At least he wasn't overweight. His lungs, however, they felt weak and raw. The adrenaline was the only thing that kept him going.

His childhood excursion out to the watchtower had been harder. The day was just beginning to die and the tall grass and brambles were mostly a foot taller than him. He could barely see two feet in front of him. On top of that, he was far more worried about his grandmother and whether or not he could actually find his destination. Thorns and branches scraped and stuck to the sides of his cheeks and his hair, which he had kept long back then, tangled and knotted in the wind. The rangers found him on the opposite end of the creek, where he waved and begged for a telephone. His grandmother's kitchen accident marked the first time in his life that he had seen more than a small droplet of blood, and his journey to the watchtower was the first major responsibility bestowed upon him besides shearing the sheep or bathing one of the dogs.

He finally saw the dark outline of the shack in the distance. He caught up to the structure and realized that the general store had been out of business for quite some time now. He could see chairs and empty shelves piled on top of one another from beyond the dusty windows. One of them had been smashed open by a rock or a broken slab of cement. It looked like teenagers had been taking pot shots at the door with their .22s. It had become porous and splintered. The payphone had also been removed from its concrete post. His efforts had been in vain. He turned back, unconscious of his stifled pace.

On his run back to the house, he decided they would have to drive the woman to the nearest hospital themselves. He knew of a hospital on the outskirts of town, but it would take them at least thirty minutes to get there if he drove fast enough.

He felt like a fool for having wasted time running to the derelict store, knowing the whole way that it would be closed. He wasn't counting on the payphone having been removed though. That had been a surprise.

The idea of having the woman in his car worried him. It would be difficult to explain how he found her to the hospital staff or the strange police officer he had met earlier that day. He briefly entertained the idea of driving out to an area where Sandy could get reception and call an ambulance. Perhaps he was being too paranoid? Either way he would have to explain why she was on his property, and the truth would be difficult to believe. There was no reason or evidence, however, to suggest that he had done anything wrong. The suddenness of the situation was hindering his ability to think clearly. He was panicking just like Sandy. As he made the last few jolts toward the light of the house, all he could think about was putting this situation behind him.

CHAPTER NINETEEN

Sandy watched Yona burst through the door. He rested his hands on his knees in the kitchen as he caught his breath.

"There's nothing there. We'll have to drive her to the hospital."

"You didn't see a payphone?"

"It's gone." He stood up and wiped his face with the sleeve of his shirt. "Come on, let's get in the truck."

Sandy turned to Elizabeth who was looking at the floor as though she were ignoring both of them.

"Elizabeth, we have to go to the hospital."

She kept staring at the floor.

"Has she been like this the whole time?"

"No, she talked quite a bit until..." She couldn't say it. She nudged Elizabeth's shoulder. "Please, we have to go to the hospital."

The woman's face was expressionless as she looked upward into Sandy's eyes.

"What's going on?" Sandy held both of Elizabeth's callused

hands. "Do you need help walking? We can carry you to the truck."

"I can carry you easily," Yona added. "You can sit anywhere you want in the truck."

She stood up slowly without any help from Sandy and stepped over to the kitchen where Yona stood. A few splotches of blood spread into the carpet, marking her trail. "Okay," she whispered.

Yona sighed in relief.

She walked to the door when her leg gave out from under her and she collapsed on the dirty tile of the entranceway. Yona rushed over her and began helping her up. She screamed and put a gash in his face with a jagged fingernail. He tried to calm her, but she continued frantically pushing him away.

Sandy could see what was happening. She latched onto his back and tried to pull him away. "You're too imposing, she's just afraid."

They finally stepped back in the kitchen, giving Elizabeth space. She curled up facing the door and cried.

Sandy hadn't heard anyone cry like that since she was ten and her parents nearly divorced. She remembered the fight in the kitchen. Both of them had been drinking as the true Irish Catholics they were. The details and reasons for the fight had been lost in the clutter and chaos of Sandy's mind, but she never let go of the sounds: the hushed, whispered arguing and the sudden shrieks as the fight became physical. Alcohol made her mother a nagging perfectionist. She would boss everyone around the apartment, making them organize and clean. Her father's drinking normally made him fun-loving and he would give them piggyback rides across the living room until his wife entered the picture and he quickly became defensive and bitter. The momentum of their last, giant fight was unprecedented. They went from bickering, to yelling, to fighting in a matter of minutes and Sandy soon heard plates breaking and chairs falling over. By the end of the night, her father had disappeared and her mother lay on a kitchen floor littered with sharp debris. She wouldn't stop crying. Sandy tried to approach her to offer comfort, but she didn't want her children to see her weakness. She screamed until Sandy left the room.

Elizabeth lay on the floor, sobbing. The humiliation and suffering in her stressed, altered voice was so close to the anguish Sandy had heard in her mother that it hurt her to listen. Yona still felt the need to act, but Sandy held him back.

"Just give her a minute," she said. "She just needs to cool down from the trauma." She didn't want to hear her cry but she knew it was necessary.

Yona stood with his hands in his pockets, watching Elizabeth as though she were a failing engine. He felt inept and useless.

Once Elizabeth's tears subsided, she pulled herself off the floor as slowly as possible. Sandy helped her up and opened the door for her. With a sudden burst of energy, she tore away from Sandy and ran back inside the house toward Yona.

Sandy screamed and Yona lifted up his hands to block himself. Elizabeth grabbed a silver letter opener from the display case on the counter and lunged at him, cursing incoherently. He fell backwards, fighting her off. He tried to grab ahold of its blunt edges of the letter opener, but her movements were too erratic. She plunged down, reopening the scar tissue in the palm of his right hand.

"Get off!" he yelled, kicking her three feet away.

She pushed herself back toward Yona, stretching out her hand. The tip of the blade plunged into his skin. He yelled in shock and pain. Sandy pulled a dusty, decorative vase from the entranceway and swung it across Elizabeth's head. The vase didn't even crack. It came down hard on Elizabeth's skull, knocking her sideways. She fell onto the carpet directly under the dining table and stopped moving.

The silver handle of the letter opener stuck out of Yona abdomen. His hands shook at his sides. He was afraid to touch it.

"I don't think she got me that good," he said, pushing his neck upward to see the damage. "Most of the thing's not even sticking in me."

It looked worse from Sandy's vantage point.

"Yona, she stabbed you."

"Yeah, she did."

"She stabbed you."

"I can see that!" he yelled. "Here, grab her and lock her in the bathroom."

Sandy hesitated.

"Do it!"

She held onto Elizabeth's legs and dragged her unconscious body into the hallway. She felt her head in the bathroom. It wasn't bleeding. She closed the door and, unable to lock it from the outside, tied the knob to the bedpost with her belt.

Yona tried to feel his wound, but it stung and he began to writhe from the pain. "Sandy, get me the rubbing alcohol."

She raced over to the living room and handed him the bottle. He winced and gritted his teeth as he crudely poured the transparent liquid onto his stomach and the puncture in his hand.

Sandy took her phone onto the patio. There was still no signal.

"Sandy!"

"What?"

"Sandy, you have to take the road into town and call an ambulance."

"We have to go together."

"No, I can't risk standing and moving around."

"I can help you into the car," she pleaded.

"No Sandy, it hurts too fuckin' much."

"What do I do?

"Just get me the bottle of polish vodka from the fridge and a pillow for my neck."

"No, no, no…You're fine."

"Sandy, stop it! You have to take your car and go to town. Call the EMS and have them ride out here, okay? There's plenty of 24-hour gas stations who will let you use the phone if you can't get a better signal."

She swallowed and suppressed her tears. "Okay, I can do it. I'll go as fast as possible."

"Don't take any risks."

"I won't."

They kissed and she gently set a pillow under his head and handed him the bottle of vodka. She stood near the doorway with her keys in hand.

"What are you waiting for?"

"What if Elizabeth wakes up?"

"Just go, Sandy."

CHAPTER TWENTY

She thought she would burst into tears, but as she steered, negotiating a hairpin turn, she was unable to make a sound. Her hands were steady and her driving focused. It didn't make any sense.

The fields on either side of her sedan's headlights appeared as nothing more than infinite, dark chasms. Occasionally, her headlights caught the beginnings of a gravel driveway leading up to a trailer or the smashed windows of an abandoned building. She wouldn't dare ask one the local residents for help. She knew it was foolish to ignore such an option, but it also seemed foolish to take the risk.

She was holding it together remarkably well, though her mind was still centered on the notion of Yona dying. That would be the last straw. She was at the mercy of a relentless and random fate, but she couldn't give up. She was still driving through the dark countryside, fulfilling her objective. Part of her felt astonished by her perseverance, astonished and gratified. She suppressed these feelings with guilt, mistaking them for narcissism.

She turned once again, finally making it out of the woodland and onto the roads that lead into town. There was a small gas station near the luminous green sign marking the miles to the nearest cities. The station's lights were on, attracting a visible mist of fluttering insects. The parking lot was modest and nearly empty except for a few old trucks and a police cruiser. She parked the sedan at an oblique angle and ran from the car without closing the door. The tarmac was new and her pink sneakers made almost no sound as she raced to the building beyond the gas pumps. The doors and windows were covered with cigarette, beer, and lottery advertisements. She swatted the gnats away before grabbing onto the sticky, metal door handle. The gasoline fumes were replaced by a thick haze of Lysol and burning tobacco. A familiar face sat on the booth near the counter. The officer from earlier was smoking a cigar with the owner of the station, tapping his ash into a giant, amber-colored ashtray.

"What can I do for you, missy?" The owner smiled from behind his white handlebar moustache. She noticed he was wearing a snake-hide bandana.

Thatcher, his skin looking far more haggard under the fluorescent lights, gave a brief chuckle. "Leave the little lady alone, Jeremy," he said.

"Ah, she's pretty tall to be a little lady."

"Jeremy!" He took a puff on the cigar. "Pay no attention to him, Ma'am."

Sandy was overwhelmed with disgust. She hated these people, these smug, ignorant people. "Call an ambulance," she said.

Thatcher's expression changed. "What's happened?"

"A woman has been tortured and traumatized. She's locked in our bathroom. She stabbed my boyfriend. They both need medical attention." Her tone of voice was calm, controlled. Her calmness perplexed them.

The owner gestured toward his phone. "Should I go ahead…?"

"Wait just a second. Aren't you the woman from the white truck and the Indian?"

"Call the fucking ambulance!" she yelled at the owner.

"Hold on!" Thatcher yelled as he stood up, placing the cigar in the ashtray. "Let's keep things in order here. You've got a girl locked in your bathroom and your boyfriend's been stabbed?"

"Yes, they both need medical attention."

"Who is this girl?"

"She was screaming in the woods. We found her." Sandy was finally panicking. "She stabbed him."

"Why was she screaming in the woods?"

"She's been hurt badly."

"By whom?"

"I don't know. You need to call an EMS. Please, you can follow me down to the house. We need help!"

Thatcher hesitated, adjusting his belt. "Are you sure you're alright?"

"What's wrong with you? He's been stabbed."

The owner raised an eyebrow and looked at him. "We should call an ambulance and follow her up there, Thatch. I don't reckon she's lying. "

"We aren't gonna call nobody all the way up here till I see this mess for myself."

"You can't be fucking serious."

"That's enough." He pushed her toward the door with

surprising strength.

"Get the hell off me!"

"Stop screaming or I will arrest you." he warned.

"Stop pushing me or I'll sue the whole county!" She called out to the store owner. "Dial 911, they're at the house off Sa-Ka-Ha-Na Road."

He gave her a dubious look as if she were speaking a foreign language.

"I just want to drive up there before we call anybody," Officer Thatcher said, trying to sound friendlier. He gently placed her in the backseat of the police car but didn't handcuff her. He sat down in the front seat and started the ignition.

"I don't mean no disrespect, I just need to see this mishap with my own eyes."

"You're an idiot," she said.

"Police have protocol. I can't just believe any hysterical woman that runs into a gas station."

"Aren't you supposed to protect and serve, take what citizen's say to be the truth?"

Thatcher nodded. "I've come to find there's a right way and wrong way to go 'bout that."

She rolled her eyes and rammed her head against the window.

"Stop that!" he said, staring at her in the rearview mirror. "Where did you say y'alls place was?"

"Take a right at Sa-Ka-Ha-Na Road. You can't miss it."

"Umhmm." He took his hat off and scratched his scalp through his jet-black hair. "Let me ask you this: How come you had to run into a gas station so far away if you needed an ambulance. Don't y'all got a phone up there?"

"It's his grandparents' house. They never had a phone."

"You see, that don't add up for me. What about a cell phone?"

She was too exhausted for the accusations. "I tried to, but we couldn't get reception." Her voice cracked as she realized how unconvincing she sounded.

Thatcher stopped talking and focused on driving.

They hit the back roads after several minutes of tense silence. There was more light on the road heading the opposite direction. She could see the outlines of the trailers and tree trunks in the moonlight. She wondered how it was possible. Her grasp of physics was less than minimal but it still felt wrong. Shouldn't the moon have illuminated the same area evenly regardless of the direction? She looked out the back window of the police car. The moon hung low and appeared orange, giving the darkness a vague tinge of sepia. She couldn't remember what caused these phenomena, or whether it had to do with the seasonal changes.

"When this is over you're going to be fired," she said.

He chose not to respond.

"You negligent, hillbilly son-of-a-bitch."

He remained silent.

Thoughts of Yona bleeding to death on the carpet continued to haunt her. Losing him meant losing her only companion, her only friend. She would be adrift with barely a place to live and no job. Where could she go? Mexico? Portland? Her sister's? She wanted to rip out the metal cage separating her form Thatcher and strangle him to death. She thought up another insult and began to scream it out until she saw the boy in the headlights.

He was wearing a green t-shirt and a pair of dirty jeans. His feet were bare and caked with red clay. He couldn't have been older than eight. She didn't get a good look at the details in his face, but she remembered his hair was shaggy and brown. He was standing at the side of the road in a leafy ditch before jumping into the middle of the double yellow lines separating the lanes. Thatcher didn't notice him.

"Look out!"

He jolted in his seat and instantly turned the wheel to the far left. The car slammed into the ditch. She opened her eyes and un-buckled her seatbelt. The headlights were destroyed but she could still see smoke rising from the engine. Thatcher held onto his seat to look at Sandy. His nose had been crushed when the airbag deployed. He asked in a wheezy voice if they had hit the kid. She didn't answer. Instead she asked him to let her out of the car. The driver's door fell open and he limped out, fumbling with his keys until finding the right one to open the back doors. Sandy stepped onto the dark road and looked for the green t-shirt.

"You have a flashlight?" she asked.

He turned it on and scanned the black stretch of road, then checked the drainage ditch and underneath the car. The boy was gone.

"I don't see him."

Sandy yelled, cupping her hands around her mouth to project the sound.

"There's no use."

She told him to shut up and continued calling. "Radio an ambulance."

Thatcher staggered back to the totaled vehicle. He covered his bleeding nose with the palm of his hand.

She continued to search the road.

"He's over here," Thatcher said. She heard him interrogating the boy. "What are you doing in the middle of the road at night?"

Sandy ran back to the police car. "Is he alright?"

A tremendous crack echoed through the woods.

"What was that?"

She received no answer. She ran faster as Thatcher's nasal voice screamed for help. At first she only saw the warped vehicle alone in the ditch. She tore through the rhododendron branches and stopped at the edge of a clearing where a group of children were mashing Thatcher's already mangled body with heavy branches. One of them held a baseball bat. His crooked bleeding hand reached out to her. The boy in the green shirt raised his head, looking directly into her eyes, and pulled out Thatcher's gun. She ran across the road, into the bushes, as the flash of three gunshots briefly illuminated the clearing.

CHAPTER TWENTY-ONE

She didn't know where she was going. She had narrowly escaped the bullets as they hissed past her, striking the gray trunk of a poplar tree. She ran at least half a mile before taking shelter behind a tall outcrop covered in wet, spongy moss and struggled to the top after sliding off on several attempts, gripping chunks of green in her fists. The view yielded no special insight or advantage. The woods looked calm, benign. No one else was coming. She could have been easily tracked by all the careless jostling, but none of the children appeared to have followed her. She couldn't hear any approaching footfalls. All she could hear were her own frantic, exhausted breaths. Once her heart rate slowed, she listened to a distant body of water; cold liquid clicking and snapping in the darkness, smoothing over piles of rocks. It was a creek, though she had no way of knowing if it was the creek, the one they called Haverbrook Creek that flowed beside the watchtower where the boy was found. She doubted that it was common to name creeks. It must have held a long forgotten significance, she thought, like the only local source of clean water during the 1920's or 30's. The name of the creek was the least of her pertinent worries, but she needed something to focus on to keep herself from screaming.

When she was certain no one was following her, she began to quietly crawl further down the ridge. She kept her head low and did her best to blend in with the tree trunks, trying to make her body seem like a giant knot of biomass, but in the sepia moonlight, she still looked like a human being wandering alone. The canopy above her blocked out the stars, allowing only stray bands of light from the moon through its jagged gaps where leaves failed to overlap and branches had fallen. Black bears were out tonight, sniffling through garbage cans and grazing on sweet grass. Raccoons and possums were scuttling across boulders and dead logs. It was spring. If she ran into a bear, there was a chance it would be accompanied by cubs. That's when lungs were ripped out and skulls were cracked.

She parted a pair of branches and stepped over a moss-covered rock to the edge of the creek. Cautiously checking her surroundings like a nervous deer, she cupped her hands in the flowing water and began to drink. The water was cold. She drank four giant mouthfuls and splashed some onto her face, washing away the congealed sweat. She felt satisfied and sat down on the rock.

What would she do from here?

The answer was simple: find a trailer or a cabin where she could use the phone and return to Yona as soon as possible.

She washed her hands in a puddle of water atop the rock and took a deep breath. She could do this. There was nothing in her way. Fate, in all its relentlessness, could be molded if she kept herself in one piece and wasted no time.

It was an easy walking path along the creek. Most of the low branches hung on the right side and the dirt was not as slick. The wind was still blowing through the trees. She could hear it tear through the leaves like a rasped whisper coupled with the faint sound of creaking, as though a branch were about to snap. She stood and looked up. The canopy still had the strange amber glow but she couldn't make out any definitive shapes.

"I'm scared," she said out loud.

Don't ...be...scared.

It was a deep, airy voice, originating from above her.

"Who's there?"

Here I am.

She imagined a pair of hiker's boots dangling before her. The shadow of a man hung above her from a rope knotted around his neck. His body moved with the wind. She fell to the ground and pushed herself back. As he moved forward, she could see part of his body. His khaki pants were caked in black mud from the side of the creek. He wore a faded denim shirt with pockets on both breasts. His face remained invisible as he steadily swung back into the shadow.

Don't go.

The whispers were so quiet, yet she heard them with perfect clarity.

"What are you?"

Alone.

"What happened?"

Death.

"Why are you still here?"

Don't know.

"Am I dead?"

No.

"But you're dead?"

Yes.

She got back on her feet but kept the same distance from the figure.

"You've been hanged."

Hanged.

"Who hanged you? Was it the children?"

No children.

"You hanged yourself."

Hanged.

"Do you have a cell phone in your pockets?"

Pockets are empty.

"Who were you?"

A man. Alone.

"Were you hiking?"

Hiking.

"Were you camping?"

Camping.

"Do you have a camping space anywhere? You know, with your gear and maybe a cell phone."

No cell phone. Up the ridge to the right in the clearing. Old tent, tarp, more rope, some food.

"I don't need food; I need to call an ambulance."

Then...I have nothing for you.

"How long have you been here?"

Since...

"Why did you hang yourself?"

Don't remember.

She didn't have anything else to say.

Thirsty. Can you bring me some water?

"I don't have a cup."

My canteen is at my feet.

She reluctantly walked beneath him. A foul odor surrounded his body. She brushed the dead leaves away with her feet and searched for the canteen.

Fell in the bush.

She searched the bush and finally spotted a silver-colored canteen. It was light and empty.

"You want me to fill this with water?

Please.

She stepped over to the creek and filled the aluminum cylinder with the cold water from a shallow end.

"There might be a little sand in it."

He said nothing.

She stepped toward him and presented the water. A colorless hand extended slowly and took the canteen. He guzzled everything. His stiff, twisted throat muscles strained and ripped as he swallowed. She heard some of it leaking out of his neck.

"Is that enough?"

The colorless hand returned the canteen.

More.

She went back to the creek and filled it once more. The water stayed inside his throat this time. When he finished, he threw the canteen back into the bush.

"I have to go now and get help."

No help.

"What do you mean?"

Have to leave here.

"Why?"

Children are not children.

"Then what are they?"

They are something else. Everywhere here is something else.

"Are they ghosts?"

Demons. Or...something else.

"Are you a demon?"

No.

"What are you?"

Alone.

"I have to go now."

Don't go.

"I have to help someone."

Stay with me.

"I can't." She walked past him. His hand immediately grabbed the back of her hair and jerked her backward. She pulled his brittle fingers apart and ran away, following the creek. His body swung in the wind.

CHAPTER TWENTY-TWO

A single word stuck in his mind. He couldn't remember its meaning or the syllables it took to write it out in Cherokee. All he could remember was the word itself: Nuh-Wa-Doe-Hee-Ya-Duh. He didn't know why this word had come to the fore of his thoughts.

He hadn't spoken so much as a few words and phrases in Cherokee since he left his grandparents' home. His grandfather called him once on a payphone when he was studying at Fluor. They spoke mostly Cherokee, adding a few technical terms and street names here and there, until the end of the conversation when it shifted exclusively to English. He couldn't remember who started it, but the talk ended in a lukewarm goodbye rather than a congenial Do-Na-Da-Guh-Huh-Yuh. Goodbye felt more cold and final when he said it. He didn't like the word goodbye, or speaking English with his grandparents. Their English was guttural and twangy. They said things like "not never" and "ain't done tooken none." They spoke their own language with strict adherence to the Kituwa tonal variations and nightmarishly complex grammar.

It was not the last time he spoke to his grandfather before the heart attack, but it was, at least for Yona, the last time they would truly communicate. They never talked about his goals or his feelings after that. They never talked about the farm. They never looked at one another face to face. Nothing had happened in their previous conversation. There was no disagreement, no harsh words. Cain had just drifted away from him. It took energy and persistence to care about a son, to wish for his well-being, to worry about him in the silent moments of his absence. Somehow, he had lost his endurance.

Yona reemerged from his thoughts, the word indelibly scraped into his skull, and looked at the letter opener in his stomach. He nursed on the vodka. It wasn't killing the pain as well as he had hoped, but with luck he would eventually pass out. He laughed and wondered why he was fate's punching bag when it came to accidents. His head leaned back and he gazed at the ceiling, which had accrued a reasonable layer of dust. He turned to the hallway and looked at the shut door of the bedroom. He hadn't heard a sound since Sandy had locked the woman inside the bathroom. She was probably dead. He didn't blame her for the wound. She was just fighting back, like a cornered animal. He drank a little more and closed his eyes, hoping he would fall asleep.

Oh-Shee-Stee-Day-Na-Da-Zoe-Hee: Nice to you meet you. Nice to meet you father death, here to take me. I have a few moments to sit here and try to achieve peace. Peace: Nuh-Wah-Doe-Hee-Ya-Duh. That was it. That was the word: harmony, peace.

CHAPTER TWENTY-THREE

A porch light glared in the distance, reflecting off the creek. From behind the bushes, she could see a moderately sized trailer home. It appeared to be well kept. There were no beer cans strewn across the lawn or chained-up attack dogs barking ferociously at every stray noise. The young man sitting in the lawn chair on the porch wore a pair of leather cowboy boots, blue jeans, and a button-up shirt. His face was cleanly shaven and his hair neatly combed to the side. He sipped on a longneck bottle of light beer.

She stood up and walked toward the light until the young man saw her.

"Jesus Christ!" His accent was distinctly Northern.

"I need to call 911. My boyfriend's been stabbed."

He discarded his drink and helped her up the steps into the trailer. It was well-decorated inside, almost as if it were a hotel room. The scent of fabric softener in the air and the violet flat-paint on the walls indicated a woman's touch, though the trailer seemed empty. It must have been a cheap timeshare of sorts for the younger crowd who couldn't afford the lakeside cabins. He sat her down on the plush couch across from the television. It was a dated appliance with its thick body and glass screen, but it would have been luxurious in the mid-90s. Her surroundings were comfortable and she suddenly felt at ease, as though the night was close to its end. She would spend the next couple of days in a hospital by Yona's side and talk to a therapist to cope with the trauma.

The young man had one brown eye and one blue eye. He was probably used to people staring at them. She didn't know for sure, but his demeanor combined with his surroundings caused her to think of him as a gay man. It comforted her to think of him as a young, gay man.

"My name's Nicholas," he said. "Have you been hurt?"

"No, my boyfriend needs an ambulance. He's been stabbed."

"Is he back up on the road?"

"No, he's back up at our house. Please, I've been through so much tonight..."

He nodded. "No, I'll get it. The phone's in the bedroom; I'll call 911." He stood up and headed toward the hallway.

She told him the address of Yona's house and he repeated it on his way to the bedroom in order to remember. She sat alone looking around the room at the decorations. It had been pulled right out of a generic home and gardening magazine. There was a banjo in the corner, an expensive elaborate banjo with mother-of-pearl etched in with the mahogany bridge. She took a small pillow from the side of the couch and held it to her chest. Nicholas walked out of the bedroom and sat down on the chair across from her.

"They're on their way," he said. "Can I get you anything, a glass of water?"

There was enough water in her system. For the first time, she realized she needed to urinate.

"Actually, can I use the bathroom? And then can you drive me home?"

"Yeah, sure." he said. "Are you from around here?"

"No, I was on...vacation." There was no shorter way to explain why she was up here.

She set the pillow back in its respective corner. As she stood up, she caught a glimpse of the kitchenette. There was a small white cordless phone on the counter near the egg timer. She pretended not to notice. She walked into the hallway and opened a towel closet.

"It's the one on the left," he said.

There was a pink rug in the bathroom and a porcelain soap dispenser shaped like a honey jar. She quietly locked the door behind her. The seat was cold and she urinated as quickly as possible, before turning the water on. She opened the small window and removed the ceramic figures from the sill.

Nicholas was on the other side of the door. "You okay in there?"

"Yeah, I'm almost ready to go."

She removed the screen and hoisted herself up.

"What are you doing in there?"

She didn't bother answering. She pulled herself halfway out of the window and saw that the drop was at least seven feet downward into a patch of sticky bushes. If she maneuvered herself around, she would be able to fall legs first.

The lock on the door suddenly popped open, as if Nicholas had a button that just as easily unlocked the door. He had a small screwdriver in his hand when he entered.

"What are you doing?"

He might have been a normal guy just trying to help, but she didn't feel like giving him the benefit of the doubt. She needed to get away. She continued to pull herself through the window.

He tossed the screwdriver in the sink and grabbed onto her legs. She began to scream "rape."

"Nobody can hear you," he said. He pulled her from the windowsill. Her body slammed against the vinyl tile and she grabbed the pink rug as she was dragged back into the living room. Nicholas stuck something sharp into her neck and she continued to scream. She fell down again knocking her head against the coffee table.

When she woke up, the room was definitely darker. The only light came from the television. She felt groggy and weightless. She knew she had been drugged. It reminded her of her college days, when she used to get stoned on Saturday evenings, only worse. She had no control over the waves of sensation attacking her nerves. She had no energy either. She wanted to get up and run again, but her legs would only shuffle against the carpet. She wasn't tied down with rope or duct tape because she didn't need to be. He had her stuck in her own body.

Sandy sat on the couch in the miniature living room nestled between two girls in identical gray dresses. Both of them had short, boyish haircuts. One girl was dark, possibly Hispanic or Indian. The other had short blonde hair and tattoos covering her arms. Both of them had bulging stomachs. She thought they were fat, but, once she saw that the weight was only carried in the middle, she realized they were pregnant.

They were pregnant young women-possibly teenaged girls-wearing the same shitty, gray dress and the same shitty, dyke hair-style, she thought.

"Where the hell did y'all come from?" she said, doing her best not to slur her words.

The girls looked at her but didn't respond. They're eyes returned to the television.

The brightness hurt Sandy's eyes, so it was hard to focus on what was being watched. The volume had been turned off.

"What the hell are we watching?" she asked.

The girls didn't react to her question.

She turned around as best she could and looked at the kitchenette. It was just two feet away from her, but it looked as though it were thirty yards out. She could barely hear Nicholas and the other man talking. The other man was a tall Indian wearing black jeans, black boots, and a tight black t-shirt. To compliment this ominous outfit, he had long, black hair tied into a ponytail with a rubber band. His face looked far darker than Yona's. It was wrinkled and creased into a perpetual scowl. Nicholas was exchanging money with him and laughing. They both drank glasses of whiskey.

She turned back around to the television and suddenly realized what they were watching. It was some smutty, horribly lit, hardcore porn film.

"Oh, give me a break," she said out loud. "Are you guys seriously watching this?"

As she expected, neither of the girls responded. The film was shot in a cheap motel room. A young girl wearing a purple wig was being blindfolded and sodomized by an unseen man.

"Turn this crap off," she yelled.

"Shut up, mule," Nicholas shouted back.

Mule? What the hell did that mean? It was hard to think she had pegged him as a gay man.

The pornography kept getting more violent. The man was choking the girl with his penis and urinating in her face as she gasped for air.

Sandy stopped watching when the boy entered the living room. It was the little boy with the green shirt. Despite the effects of the drugs, her adrenaline began to flow. She watched him walk over to the Indian who picked him up as if he were his son or nephew.

She had walked right back into the lion's den.

Nicholas walked over in front of the television and turned it off, breaking the pregnant girls' trance.

"Alright guys, movie night's over."

The Indian man clapped his hands and said, "Back in the truck." The two obliged, running out the door.

Sandy looked at both men, wondering where the boy had gone.

"You want to check her and see if she's good?" asked Nicholas.

"I don't know...she's got pretty wide hips. Shouldn't take long to break her. You said she's not from 'round here, right?"

Nicholas turned to her. "Are you on the pill?"

She didn't answer.

He sighed and unzipped her pants.

"No!" she screamed.

Both men became angry with what they saw. Nicholas zipped her back up. He walked to the kitchen and pulled a revolver from the cabinet. "I'll give you the money back."

"That's life," the Indian said, indifferently.

Sandy did her best to fight as he pulled her into the kitchen and forced a plastic bag over her head. The boy in the green shirt sat at the kitchen table looking excited. She begged him not to kill her. She said she'd do anything. He pushed her head to the bottom of the sink. She pleaded with him and offered him any sexual favor he wanted. He pressed the barrel of the gun to her head and pulled the hammer back.

"Wait a minute," the Indian said. "Give me half of my money back. I know some guys I can sell her to and still make a profit."

"Who?"

"The Carter boys."

He lifted the gun up and clicked the hammer back in place. "They'll still take her with a dick?"

"I don't have to tell him. They'll probably chop it anyway, just don't tell nobody. He's got a good pair of breasts and a working asshole. That's all those mongrels'll give a goddamn about."

"Whatever you want, man." He ripped off the bag and threw her to the floor.

Her slack body collapsed.

"Ain't nobody looking for her, right?"

Nicholas returned the gun to the cabinet. "Nah, her boyfriend's bleeding to death somewhere."

"You stabbed him?"

"I don't know how it got done. I'd guess one of the sprouts did it."

"Alright, then." The Indian man hoisted Sandy over his shoulder as she writhed and fought his grasp. There was a giant, black ford truck parked in the dirt lot. The two girls sat in the backseat. She was thrown into the bed. The side of her face hit a stray toolbox. He produced a pair of handcuffs and tightly bound her wrists, then spread a blue tarpaulin over her body. The cuffs sliced into her skin. She kept screaming but the sound of the engine was too overpowering. Eventually, her voice became dry and hoarse. She could barely make a sound.

CHAPTER TWENTY-FOUR

Yona opened his eyes when he heard a sound coming from the bedroom. It was the girl. She was periodically thrashing her body against the bathroom door, trying to get out. He wished she were dead. He wondered if he could crawl to the door and do it himself to buy time. He decided against it. He needed his gun. The shells to the shotgun were hidden away in the top shelf of the closet. There was no way he would be able to reach them. Come to think of it, he hadn't fired the shotgun in nearly ten years. The powder in the shells had probably lost a significant amount of potency. He could see the buckshot backfiring directly into his face as he pulled the trigger. There was another option: the two revolvers in the basement. The bullets were in a trick compartment on the bottom of the box. The only problem was getting into the basement.

He moved his legs and extended his arms out, gripping the rug. He began to push himself as slowly as possible. His gut was searing. It felt like his stomach was ripping open. The metal inside him seemed to lower into his body. He knew nothing about abdominal wounds, but took the chance anyway. He didn't want the blood to coagulate around the letter opener. It felt like more damage was being done. After a few moments of hesitation, he plucked the silver handle from his stomach. A thin line of fresh blood seeped down his shirt as he clenched his teeth, trying to let the pain settle. He threw the letter opener down the stairs to the basement door and continued pulling himself across the floor. It was difficult to tell whether or not he made the right decision. He would figure that out in the hospital, if he made it that far.

The journey to the foot of the stairs was agonizing. Though he wasn't bleeding profusely, his blood had smeared across the floor, marking his trail. The girl in the bathroom was making progress. As she persisted to smash against the door, he could hear the rope snapping cracking.

CHAPTER TWENTY-FIVE

The tarpaulin was lifted. Two young men in faded white shirts stared at her.

"Oh, she's a redhead. That's special," one of them said. He was wearing a worn baseball cap.

The other had a shaved head. He spat in the dirt before asking, "How much?"

The Indian walked around the back of the truck as he adjusted his belt. He pulled his hair out and refitted the ponytail with the rubber band, before offering them cigarettes. They took them without thanking him and lit them with their own lighters. She noticed how their faces scrunched as they smoked.

"I'll give her to ya for a hundred flat."

That's how much her life was worth to him.

The one with the shaved head was in charge of making the decisions. He ran his fingers along his rough chin. He reminded her of Thompson, the kid who cost her the Palmetto Tech job. He bit his upper lip and fished out his wallet.

"She a screamer?"

"Yeah, but you can just put a rag in her mouth or glue it shut," the Indian suggested.

The young man in the baseball cap stared into the truck. "Can't we buy none of them?"

"You just wanna fuck somebody pregnant, Jay?"

"You always keep the best for yourself. What kind of whore-house you runnin' up there on the mountain?"

The other looked at him and punched him in the stomach. "Shut up. Ain't none of our business. Help me with the bitch."

They each grabbed onto Sandy's pants and threw her from the truck bed. She landed on soft ground.

"Can we keep the cuffs?"

"They're all yours." The Indian jumped back into the truck and drove up the ridge. Gradually, the light faded from the forest. She was dragged by her shoulders through the water and across an embankment that split the creek into two streams. She fought them as best she could but the effects of the drug, or drugs, were still powerful and crippling. She would have to save her energy for the right moment to get away. With this in mind, she knew she would have to deal with a certain amount of humiliation and pain until that moment came. The young man with the shaved head tossed his cigarette away. She saw a hunting knife in a leather holster fitted to his belt. They brought her to a rundown double-wide beneath several oak trees.

"Where do you want her?"

"Put her on the kitchen floor."

Jay, the larger one with the baseball cap, pushed her inside and kicked her onto the floor.

"You guys have no idea how rich I am. I'll pay you to let me go. I'll keep it all quiet."

"I've heard that one." He smiled and opened the cabinet under the sink. With aggressive precision, he wrapped an entire role of duct tape to her wrists and the handcuffs binding them, grafting her to the plumbing.

"Probably should've asked him for the key," he said.

She felt the sticky floor on her back. The ceiling was caked in urine-colored nicotine stains. Jay's boots made a sucking noise as he walked to the refrigerator, pulling up several years' worth of spilled beer and cola. He popped open a beer on the wall and discarded the cap as it rolled under the dining table.

"I'll fuckin' kill you," she said.

Jay spewed a mouthful of beer at her. Some of it hit her jeans but the rest splashed against the countertop. He was keeping his distance. They had done this before. He knew she would try jamming her foot into his crotch if she had the chance. Blowjobs and kisses where probably off-limits too, but she knew what to do just in case.

The bald, slender young man walked inside. He tossed a jar of petroleum jelly into the puddle of beer froth on the counter.

"Ah hell man, you gotta tape her feet down."

"You gotta get her pants off first."

"What? You want me to do it?"

"I ain't going near her without you."

They dove on top of her and sat on her legs. She was too weak to fight back. Jay unzipped her jeans. They immediately noticed the bulge before peeling back the last article of clothing to stare at her limp penis and testicles.

"Well, fuck me." He flicked her left testicle with his finger, sending an electrical pain through her body.

She gritted her teeth and spat what little saliva she had left at their faces.

"I think that timber nigger son of a bitch just stole our money. That's why he couldn't use her for himself."

"We'll get'em next time," Jay said. "But I ain't letting nothing go to waste. Turn her over."

They turned her around and ripped off her pants. Her arms twisted in their sockets and pressed against her cheeks. Her testicles, still throbbing with pain, pressed against the floor. Jay taped her legs down. She could feel the abdominal muscles stretching in her contorted body. She was stuck now. In the corner of her eye, she watched the slender young man smear a palm full of jelly onto him. All she could think about was Yona, lying on the carpet without color in his face.

A tremendous blast echoed through the forest beyond the trailer as the flimsy window above the sink shattered. She thought she had heard a car crash or a sledge hammer pound against a slab of sheet metal. She strained her neck to look to the right. The wall and side of the refrigerator were covered in splotches of viscous blood and shards of pure, white bone matter. She watched the nearly decapitated body fall flat on its back, its pants still dropped around the ankles. It was all followed by the unmistakable sound of a lever ejecting a round from a long-range firearm. Jay rushed to the living room and grabbed a small handgun from a box beneath an armchair. Another thunderous shot ripped through the wall and hacked off the side of his arm. He screamed as blood came gushing from a main artery. The last shot tore through his chest, permanently forcing him into a sitting position against the wall.

Sandy listened to the footfalls crackling through the brambles and dead leaves. They drew closer, casually rustling along the dirt and up the front steps of the double-wide. Someone forced the front door open and entered the kitchen. She couldn't twist her neck to make another painful turn, so she stared at the floor.

"Please, don't hurt me," she said between sobs. "My boyfriend needs an ambulance. He's going to die if don't get out of here." She felt a blade run by her legs and the duct tape swiftly tear from her skin. The same happened to her wrists and her arms, but she was not yet at ease.

"These guys don't have a key for the handcuffs," she said. She felt two hands smear the petroleum jelly around her wrists. "No, I can't do this." Whoever was helping her wasn't listening. Her hands were pulled through the cuffs, slicing into her flesh. She felt the warm blood seeping down her arms. She closed her eyes and clenched her teeth. The pain remained once she was free. She lay on the floor for several minutes, afraid to look at the dead bodies of her captors and the face of the ruthless Samaritan.

CHAPTER TWENTY-SIX

He held onto the banister and lowered himself down the stairs. Each wooden plank scraped against his tailbone and spine. It was almost like rappelling. He might as well have been rappelling down a cliff for all the effort he was putting into it.

The hole in his stomach was bleeding faster. The stain in the side of his shirt was growing.

He lowered himself further and tried to scoot downward on his side. The planks bruised his hips. The banister suddenly broke from its hinges. It felt like a tree branch snapping in his hands. He fell down the remainder of the steps and landed on the cold, grimy floor of the basement. He slammed the door shut with his feet. There was no lock.

CHAPTER TWENTY-SEVEN

A woman stood over her, offering a hand. She was an Indian. Her hair was gray and cut at her shoulders. She wore a green flannel shirt around her slender body, black pants, and worn leather boots fitted tightly to her legs with buckles and straps. She stared with an expression of empathy, but Sandy refused to trust it. Her eyes were thin and punctuated by deep crow's feet unlike the rest of her olive skin, which still appeared youthful. When Sandy refused her hand, the woman calmly knelt down and placed her hunting knife back into her boot and adjusted the strap that held the Winchester across her shoulder.

"You have to come with me." The old woman pulled a roll of gauze from her short pocket and wrapped Sandy's wrists.

She wasn't going anywhere. Once her wrists were covered, Sandy pulled her underwear and pants back on and darted past her. She leapt out of the trailer. The old woman followed her but kept a distance.

"Don't go that way," she said.

Sandy barely heard her. She followed the creek, trying to maintain her balance. The woman quickly stepped to her side and helped her stand.

"Get away from me," she said.

"I want to help you and your boyfriend, but you have to stay with me. You're still drugged. If you run out into the woods here they'll just find you again. I know this place. I can help you, but we have to get those drugs out of your system, okay?"

Sandy fell to her knees. "How can I trust you?"

"You don't have a choice, honey."

She started crying uncontrollably. The woman took a knee and placed her hand on her shoulder.

"Listen, I understand the trauma you're probably feeling, but if you don't keep quiet and pick yourself up, your boyfriend will probably die and the sprouts will probably find us and kill us too."

"What...the fuck...are sprouts?"

"The things that look like children? You haven't run into them yet?"

She nodded erratically.

"Okay, then you know what they're like. Now stand up and follow me."

She mustered the last ounce of energy and followed the woman up and along the ridge. She heard thunder in the distance and could almost see clouds forming in the sky.

"Shit," the old woman said. "I knew that wind earlier was a bad sign."

Something moved behind the bush. She pushed Sandy behind the tree and whipped out the rifle. A raccoon hissed and crawled up a tree.

"Guh-lee," said Sandy.

The woman looked at her. "You speak Cherokee?"

"Just a few words."

She set the rifle back to her shoulder and moved forward.

"Where are we going?"

"Dee-quay nuh-suh-ee gay-gah."

Sandy sat near a small fire pit chiseled from the stone of the outcrop. A camouflage tarpaulin held by four bamboo sticks kept her dry from the rain. She wrapped herself in a Mexican blanket and prodded the fire with a twig covered in lichen. Behind her, the woman was rummaging through the small clapboard shack, emerging from the candlelight with a jug of water. She handed it to Sandy.

"Drink," she said. "Flush those drugs out of your system."

"The guy's name was Nicholas. What did he puff me with?"

"God knows. At least, you're alive."

Sandy swigged the water and then asked her, "You live up here on this mountain?"

"Sometimes. I also have a place on the Tennessee border, a small trailer off the beaten path. I use it like a safe house."

"Who are these people? The girls...do they give birth to the sprouts?"

The old woman massaged the bridge of her nose. "This is a conversation best had with a straight head," she said. She stood up and briefly walked through the rain into the shack. Sandy waited for her, still eager to ask a slew of questions. She came back with a plate of jerky and a small bag of M&Ms.

Sandy stared at the plate. "Candy?"

"They were created for the army as a portable source of quick energy."

"It's empty calories."

"Well, that's what the jerky is for. You need protein. Don't tell me you're a fuckin' vegetarian."

Sandy ate a handful of the chocolates. "No, I'm not."

They ate as the rain continued to pour. The blanket became too hot for her and she spread it around her crossed legs.

"I appreciate you helping me, but I don't have a lot of time," she said.

"No, I suppose you don't."

"My boyfriend is hurt, a woman's stabbed him. She's locked in our bathroom." She thought about Elizabeth and the letter opener sticking from Yona's stomach. "Her vagina was sewn shut. Did those people have anything to do with it?"

"Yes," the woman said. "I've seen it before. It's a ritualistic thing for women in their cult who can't have children."

"It's a cult?"

"It's a little more than that."

"There was another Cherokee man. He wore all black. He's the one who sold me to those pieces of shit."

"He's not Cherokee," the woman said. "His name is Jack Caulfield. He's from the West, the desert. I'm not sure where exactly."

"What's he doing here?"

"Expanding the franchise. They travel to places, special places, to try and shift the land."

"Shift the land?"

"The energy is stronger in certain places on earth, stronger for... it's difficult to explain."

Sandy tore off a piece of jerky. "Is he some kind of witch?"

"It's almost like that, I guess," she said. "Sometimes we see faces of enemies on our friends. Most times it's the other way around. I know it sounds like horseshit, but you can't afford not to know. The group he runs is a sort of brotherhood. They follow a lot of ancient mystic rituals and do a lot of...despicable things. He's a manipulator and a businessman above all else. Don't be fooled."

"What? Is he like Charles Manson or Eric Rudolph?"

"I think he's a little smarter, but you're on the right track." She ate a handful of M&Ms. "These woods are some of the most isolated active areas. They've been touched by a kind of otherworldly force. The group lives here full time now. They have their hands in prostitution, drugs...all sorts of things. That's how they make money."

"What's with the pregnant girls and the children?"

"The women are like slaves. They're whole purpose is to give birth to the children: the sprouts."

Sandy pushed the plate away. "This is so fucked up."

The old woman laughed. "If only you knew."

She thought about the missing children and the boy found in the creek. "Do they kidnap children too?"

"The sprouts are not really children. They believe them to be possessed by...whatever forces they use. In my opinion, they're the souls of animals, demons maybe. Some dark force fills these children they give birth to and replaces the souls. That's the only way I can explain it."

"You're kidding me. You're fucking kidding me."

Sandy went silent. She couldn't stop thinking about Yona. "What do you have to do with all this?" she eventually asked.

"I protect people."

"You've done a pretty shitty job so far."

The woman lowered her head and tossed an M&M down the mountain. "Yeah well, I'm just one person. I'm lucky I've survived. I had to protect my family for a long time."

"Did they not make it?"

"Oh, they made it." She pulled a short, hand-rolled cigarette from a small pouch and lit it with a smoldering twig.

Sandy felt no urge to ask her for one. "We need to help my boyfriend."

"That's what I was meaning to talk to you about. How long have you been away from him?"

"I have no idea. I've blacked out already tonight."

"We'll assume it's been awhile," she said. "You have to see how he's doing now, so we don't waste time."

"Do you have a car?"

"There's a faster way."

Sandy raised an eyebrow.

"What's your name?"

"Sandy."

"Well Sandy, you are what we would call a two-spirited person. You're not native but that's hardly the important thing."

"What are you talking about?"

"Have you ever heard of shamanic journeying?"

"Yeah, I used to do it all the fucking time in college when I'd drop acid," she said.

The woman chose to ignore the remark. "You have both a male and a female spirit. This is very special."

"I'm just trans."

"No, you have significant advantages for traveling beyond your body. You can travel back to your boyfriend to see how he's doing."

Sandy stood up. "You're insane like everybody else here and I don't have time for this shit. You wanna protect me? Shoot the kids while I call an ambulance for my boyfriend."

"You have to trust me, Sandy."

"I don't even know who the fuck you are!"

"My name is Ama Bridger and I am the only person who can really help you."

Sandy stopped and watched her take a drag on the cigarette. "Water? You were born in a bathtub, so Mabel named you Water."

"You see? You can do more than you realize."

"No, it has nothing to do with this shaman bullshit. I've heard of you. Yona said you were dead."

Ama sighed. "Oh, Jesus. Small world, huh?"

"Yona thought you were dead all this time."

"Are you dating him?"

"Yes."

"Then I'll explain all of this to you later, but you need to open your mind and let me guide you to him first."

"No, I'm not doing anything. I'm done with this shit."

Ama kept walking closer. Sandy knew she still had a knife in her boot. She stepped backward into the rain.

"You just need to calm down."

Sandy didn't answer. She kept moving away from her.

"Sandy..."

She kept her eyes on the boot.

"Sandy..."

"What?"

"This rock is slippery." She suddenly pulled a piece of a vine from the ground in a whipping motion. Sandy immediately felt her legs give and she fell backward, plummeting downward with the raindrops.

FUCKING BITCH! I'M GONNA DIE!

and water slow droplets barely moving not moving some moving yes movement simply there cold translucent capsules of dull blue light some gray everything upside down the trees upside downblack small bits of green darkness foliage body like hanging sack some weightvery little I'm falling but I'm not falling suspension near slab of moss stone a single featherdrifting fluttering I'm slowly falling down this mountain like a goddamn feather and the raincold small bitstapping onto skin The rain and everything else has stopped moving hands on fire no weight neck lurching backward hands extended adrenaline ceased body completely calm horizontal feet scraping the side of the rock

walking walking down handscatching raincool touchearth soft invisible shadow skyblack I just walked down a fucking cliff

.................run, runtrees warped, adrenaline beginning earth moving under feetmud spattering the rocks transparent the trees transparent the earth transparent abandoned buildings transparent the frame a lone deer moving muscles trembling a crow a coyote digging on the bank a possum claws etched into the telephone poll the earth falling under the sky the rain the moon sepia covered in cloud body dug into gravelearth stopped body suspended the house I'm here I'm at the housethe house lights one truck white the door open slowly the inside Yonano Where is he? follow streak deep new red faint along to stairs railing snapped door shut at bottom there's no way in hell any of this is real the door opens slowly andlight dim blood grim wet Yona loading revolver NO! NO!

FUCKING NO! HE'S GONNA KILL HIMSELF! YONA LISTEN TO ME DON'T DO THIS I'M HERE WITH YOU NOW PLEASE DON'T DO THIS I CAN'T LIVE WITHOUT YOU YOU CAN STILL MAKE IT PLEASE I KNOW I'VE DONE AWFUL BUT I CAN STILL HELP YOU IT'S JUST A FUCKING ABDOMINAL WOUND SHE DIDN'T EVEN STAB YOU THAT BAD DON'T DO THIS I HATE YOU I HATE YOU I FUCKING HATE YOU YOU CAN'T LEAVE ME HERE WITH THESE PEOPLE I NEED YOU PUT THE BULLET BACK IN THE BOX PUT IT BACK PUT IT BACK YOU FUCKING PIECE OF SHIT NO! I LOVE YOU HOW COULD YOU GIVE UP ON ME THAT EASY I'M NOT DEAD I SWEAR GODDAMNIT YONA! CAN'T YOU HEAR ME? sound loud thrashing metallic? wooden? sound door burst behind bodyblood on legs on footprints on steps on dress on face Elizabethknife in hand Yona raised pistol

Sandy opened her eyes. She was lying on her side. Rain pelted her face. Her cheek rested on a spongy growth of moss while the rest of her was sprawled out against more rock. She pulled herself up and felt everything. She had no cracked ribs, no bones sticking out of her jeans. She didn't even feel bruised. In fact, she felt fantastic, like waking up after a full night's worth of sleep. She looked up and saw the cliff. The side of the camouflage tarpaulin flapped in the wind. Ama Bridger emerged from behind a few trees, tossing her the jug of water. She caught it.

"Whadja see?"

"Yona was going to kill the woman who stabbed him. He shot

her. I thought he was going to kill himself."

"Was he in danger?"

"She had a knife."

"That'll do it."

Sandy looked up at the cliff again. "Did I just fall from there?"

"All thirty-one feet or so."

"How am I not dead?" Ama sat down next to her. "I could've died."

Ama shook her head. "No, I put a little boost in the water I gave you. It sort of propels the journey."

Sandy pointed to the jug.

"No, that one's clean."

"I don't think I need any more drugs in my system."

"It's not exactly the same stuff."

"How does this work?"

"Only on a journey can one soul travel through the earth and the other protect the body. A two-spirited person can sit down and meditate in a war zone and wake up alive."

"This is absolutely fuck-nuts insane."

"Come on, you said Yona's alive. We have to help if we want him to stay that way."

She gave Sandy a poncho and a handgun, which she kept wedged in her small, jean pocket. They followed an old path leading up to the main road.

"Jack showed up when I was just a girl," she said. "He was charming and had a lot to say on mysticism and action against the government and Bureau of Indian Affairs. I knew he was a bit of a bullshitter, saying he had met with Russell Means and all, but I liked him. I was young."

Sandy brushed her soaked bangs behind her ears. "So that's

how you know him."

"I probably know him better than anybody else. I'm still his wife."

"You married him?"

"Yeah, I married the bastard."

"I almost got married to a girl named Alex in college. She was a dominatrix."

Ama laughed. "Her and Jack would probably get along."

"He tied you up?"

"It was what it was. When he started putting together his group of occultists, I got pregnant."

"With Yona?"

"Yup. He was supposed to be the first sprout."

Sandy stopped walking and rested against a tree. "This Jack guy is Yona's dad?"

"Yeah."

"Why isn't he like them?"

"Because his grandparents protected him from this darkness that Jack wanted."

"He didn't have his soul replaced."

"Exactly."

"Why the hell are they called sprouts?"

"Because they come from Jack's beanstalk."

Sandy cringed. "He said his dad was a white truck driver from Montana."

"That's what my parents told him."

"Why exactly did you have the grandparents raise him the whole time?"

"Jack knew I was pregnant. I ran away and kept the entire pregnancy from him to protect Yona. I went back into the woods to kill him after Yona was born, but he'd gotten strong then. He nearly killed me. I was always afraid he'd find Yona after that, so I left him there. "

"So you never saw your son again?"

"No, I visited him all the time, until my parents disowned me. I protected their house. I followed him almost everywhere. I'd walk down to the store and buy him whatever he wanted. He'd go outside to play and I'd stop by and see him for hours when my parents weren't watching him."

"Did you tell him who you were?"

"I was too afraid."

Sandy changed the subject. "What kind of shit is Jack involved with?"

"What do you mean?"

"You said it was like a cult. I mean how much deeper does it go beyond the children and the girls?"

"Ritual killings...snuff films...black magic. It's all about power. He has a whole network, mostly concentrated here in North Carolina, but he keeps in contact with these Satanist groups and other people sometimes. He used to know a guy who claimed to be a vampire. You ever hear about that guy who tried to become governor of Minnesota, called himself the Impaler?"

Sandy continued walking. "Why couldn't you kill him?"

Ama paused and stared at her feet for a while. "There were a few times when I thought I did," she said. "I could never get too close. If I got too close to Yona, Jack would find out at some point and use it against me, to torture me. If I got too close to him, somehow, someway, I knew I'd end up dead. Shit!"

"What is it?"

"I forgot to give you this." She handed Sandy a small necklace with a bone tied to the end. "Wear this."

"Will it protect me?"

"No, it wards off mosquitoes and really compliments your eyes."

Sandy pulled down the hood to her poncho and stretched the necklace over her head. "Thanks."

A shape moved across a hill in the distance. Ama pulled out her rifle.

"Did you see that?"

"I didn't see it, but I heard something."

"It was a shadow," said Sandy. "I know I saw something. It was up on that hill there."

They knelt down behind a dead tree trunk. Ama took aim, resting the barrel on the soft wood.

"Was it one of the kids?"

"No, it was bigger."

They ran along the worn path, keeping their heads low, and hid under a rhododendron tree. Nothing was following them as far as they could see. A sudden gust of wind kicked up a wave of wet leaves startling Ama. Her finger slipped on the trigger and a burst of orange flame erupted from the rifle. The bullet tore into a nearby oak, splintering the wood.

"Ah, shit."

Sandy had ducked down and covered her head with her arms. She cautiously lifted her chin, looking at the visible smoke rising from the Winchester as Ama ejected the shell and reloaded.

"We have to move. They definitely saw where that came from."

They both ran the final stretch of the trail and stopped at the edge of the road. Something was rustling the leaves behind them.

"There's a shed up the road," Ama whispered into Sandy's ear. "Follow me."

The entity behind them stayed along the side of the road under the cover of the bushes. Ama stopped only once to fire at it. Beyond them was a small concrete structure covered in vines with a rusted tin roof.

"In there!"

"Are you sure?"

"No."

They ran inside and slowly closed the wooden door without making a sound. The building was once a bathroom rest stop. Small bands of milky light penetrated the dusty, pollen-covered windows. There was a single bathroom faucet near a soap dispenser and a tilted, cracked mirror. The tile floor was covered in slimy filth and scraps of wet newspaper. Everything else appeared invisible, hidden in darkness. Sandy watched Ama pull a small piece of chalk from her poncho and draw several unfamiliar symbols on the back of the door. She thought hiding in here was a terrible idea, but she wasn't sure if she could have kept running. Her calves and joints ached. She wondered if she would ever throw up.

Three footsteps sounded outside the door followed by exhausted, animal-like breathing and sharp scratching. Ama had her rifle ready. The entity steadily walked away until its steps faded.

"What was that?"

"Does it matter?" said Ama. "Let's stay in here a little while longer." She sat down on the slick tile and propped herself against the door. Sandy squatted in the back where Ama could almost not see her. She was a murky shape in the dark.

"What the hell did you write on the door?"

"Protection."

"Just stop with the hermetic, Indian bullshit and explain it to me."

"It's witchcraft. Okay? It's fuckin' witchcraft. Are you satisfied?"

Sandy didn't reply. She felt an inexplicable chill in her neck and the muscle become tense. She looked to her side and saw a blue hand with white, transparent fingernails above raw, purple flesh grabbing onto her shoulder. Before she could scream, it had her pulled into the very last stall.

"Sandy!" Ama ran after her, kicking open the stall.

A young boy held Sandy by the neck. There was no color in his face. Tufts of his hair were missing giving his scalp a mangy, diseased appearance. Part of his cheek had been torn open, exposing his blue gums and dark, yellowing teeth.

"What do you want?"

"The...mons..ster's outside...isn't it?" He spoke with a deep gargle as cloudy water dripped from his mouth and onto Sandy's poncho.

"Whatever it is that you're afraid of, it's gone now," she said. "Let her go."

The boy tightened his grip and Sandy began to cough.

"I won't be alone any...more," he said.

"Spirit, I recognize your torment. But I need you to let my friend go. If you do this, you will save many lives."

"No...she can't go...or else the monster'll find me."

"Let her go."

Sandy managed to wheeze, "Fuck this" before pulling out her hand gun and firing it between the boy's eyes. His soft, bloodless head split down the middle, leaving his lower jaw exposed. A shrill, guttural yell erupted from the boy's apparently intact vocal chords. He fell to the floor and crawled into the corner like a maimed animal.

Ama chagrined. "That was wrong of you."

"I don't care."

"Let's go."

"Is it safe outside?"

"It's not safe in here."

"What the hell was that thing outside?"

"You've your necklace?"

"Yeah, and a lot of good it's done me."

Ama walked outside. Sandy waited a few minutes until she heard the child crawling out of the corner. She caught up with Ama along the road.

CHAPTER TWENTY-EIGHT

The sun began to rise in the distance, but the woodland was still pitch black. The house on the odd hill near the plain was silhouetted against the pre-dawn sky. Ama and Sandy cautiously opened the front door. Dried, brown splotches and streaks of blood lead them to the basement stairs. Sandy hesitated before looking down. There was mass of red were Elizabeth had once been. The blood dripping from between her legs and the gash on her head had coagulated onto the old wood.

It was real. Everything that had happened to Sandy, everything she had seen in the vision was real. They stepped over the stain and entered the basement. Yona was asleep in the corner still holding the gun. Ama carefully took it from his hand before waking him up.

He smiled faintly. "Sandy."

"I'm so sorry I left you like this."

"I had a dream you were here." His face was pale and his brow covered in sweat.

"We're gonna get you out of here, Yona. Okay?"

"That's not too bad," he said, resting his eyes.

"Where's Elizabeth's body, Yona?"

"Hmm?"

"Her body? You shot her right? She had a knife."

"I didn't shoot her. I was gonna, but she backed off and left me in the basement. How do you know that?"

"I'll tell you later, just...where is she?"

"Outside with the guy."

"The guy?"

"Yeah, a guy came down here said he'd get me an ambulance. Elizabeth ran away from him and he took off to get her back. Hope she didn't"-he gasped for a breath-"stab him too."

"Where did he go after her?"

Yona languidly pointed to the door at the back of the basement, leading to the field. The metal slab and shelf had been removed. Ama stood up and gripped her rifle. Sandy stopped her.

"Let's get Yona in the truck. Then leave it to me."

She nodded.

"Okay, Yona, we're going to try to lift you up. Can you stand?"

"I can...try." He was nodding off for short periods.

They set his arms over their shoulders and lifted up. They were so much shorter, making everything impossible. His legs couldn't extend completely, shifting his massive weight onto Ama and Sandy. They dragged him like a pair of mules carrying a broken wagon. Sandy felt her neck crush under his massive, sharp elbow like a rough, wooden yoke. Her legs trembled. Her midsection ached. She kept focusing on getting Yona out, moving step by step. Her ankles felt stiff. She couldn't allow herself to collapse. Yona's eyes opened and closed several times. He was trying to stay awake. He must have felt too nauseated to fall asleep completely. They'd get him on his back again, she thought. Then he could rest. She looked to see how Ama was doing. Her legs quivered as well and she breathed in short, pneumatic huffs. They had brought him a distance of barely seven feet. The door was another four feet away. They could make it. They had to. Sandy kept moving along, tapping into her body's reserve. She pushed Yona along, fighting the weakness in her legs, using her arms as much as possible. They finally got him outside and the incline evened out their dissimilar heights. It wasn't far now to his truck. She looked out to the field and saw a figure working with a long tool. She thought of the scythe laying in the tall grass and pictured Nicholas or Jack Caulfield chopping up Elizabeth's body. At least she knew where he was. Yona did what he could to carry himself along the last few feet to the truck. He collapsed in the backseat and thanked them before allowing himself to fall asleep. Ama massaged her neck and her shoulders.

"Did you see the man with the shovel out there?"

Sandy was relieved that it had not been the scythe, though she wasn't completely sure. "I'll get rid of him. Wait here." She thought it was strange that Ama didn't stop her. She walked across the field with her hand on her gun, closing in on the figure.

Nicholas was holding a shovel. He was digging a shallow grave as the morning light began to tear through the clouds. Birds were chirping and rustling in the tree line. He worked diligently, and had already created a mound of fresh earth near Elizabeth's corpse. Sandy walked up behind him in the wet tall grass. She held out her gun and cleared her throat to get his attention. He dropped the shovel and turned around.

"Hands up."

He raised his hands.

Sandy couldn't help but look at Elizabeth's dead body. Nicholas had slashed her throat open like a second mouth. Her entire chest was caked in dark, pungent blood.

"Did you sew her vagina?"

"The sprouts did," he said, smiling.

"Throw your gun on the ground."

He tugged the revolver from his back pocket and tossed it in the open grave.

"Put your hands back up."

Her father had once taken her to the gun range. It was another attempt to man his son up, get Sandy into the football team, the soccer team, and everything else she had no interest in. They stood side by side after the gun safety course and shot at black silhouettes of bald men. She exhausted from the noise, the stench of gunpowder, the mutual distrust. She, in her young man's body now in a painful and unwanted puberty, held the gun to her father and pulled the hammer back. She would shoot him. Put a hole straight through his sunglasses. Immediately, she turned the barrel away and set the gun down on the carpeted tray where she kept her loose ammunition. They were kicked out and banned from the range. He screamed at her on the drive home. He threatened to send her to a military school. He grabbed his testicles, yelling, "You got any balls? You got balls like these?"

Why had she pointed the gun at him? Why had she chosen to act on that mild impulse? The gun was raised, but her face was lost, confused. Her body was acting beyond her mind. She could never remember why she had done it. She just remembered the consequences.

Sandy stared at Nicholas and fired a bullet straight through his forearm. She shot him again, aiming for his chest but hitting him in the throat. It seemed fitting. He gasped as blood slowly oozed from his neck onto his white shirt. He fell into the grave, trying to stifle the bleeding by covering the hole with his hands. It looked like he was choking himself. Blood gushed over his knuckles. Sandy grabbed onto Elizabeth's stiff legs and set her body on top of Nicholas as blood began to spurt from his mouth. He managed to gargle a scream as she buried them one shovel of dirt at a time.

CHAPTER TWENTY-NINE

The sunlight only hit the tops of the trees, giving the foliage a surreal, yellow glow like the overexposed half of a Polaroid photograph. Sandy drove the truck along the road. Ama had her Winchester under the seat. She held her hand out the window.

"I haven't been in a car in almost twenty years."

Sandy didn't respond.

Ama studied her face and said, "Killing takes the wind out of you doesn't it?"

Sandy briefly made eye contact with her.

"It's different to kill someone up close, intimate, slow. When you fear for your life, when everything slows down and you fight just to survive till the next second, it doesn't feel like anything. You figure you're lucky. But taking your time, breathing it in, killing to kill, taking vengeance...part of you gets lost doesn't it?"

"Did you see me bury Nicholas and the girl?" she asked.

Ama smiled. "I had a bead drawn on him the whole time, just in case. But you didn't need my help did you? You just buried that son of a bitch."

"I didn't feel anything when I shot the kid."

"The kid was already dead. You just tormented a spirit further. This was different. This was personal wasn't it?"

"Of course it was personal. He almost killed me. He sold me to Jack Caulfield!"

Ama took out another hand-rolled cigarette. She punched the car lighter in and waited. When it finally popped out, she lit the twisted paper tip with the red coil and began to smoke. "So now you feel wrong about doing it?"

"I watched blood coming out of his throat and threw a dead body on top of him. I buried him before he had time to die. That's what I feel..."

"Guilt? From your malice? From your contempt?"

"Yes," she said. "That's about it."

Ama patted her on the shoulder. "That's how you know you're still a good person. If ever you feel you're losing your soul, at least you still have one to lose."

"Cherokee wisdom?"

"Charles Bukowski." Ama flicked the joint into the dewy grass.

Sandy eyed the glove compartment. There was a full pack of Yona's cigarettes behind the registration.

"Could you open the glove compartment and get me a cigarette?"

Ama tore the plastic off the pack and tapped the top of the box against her fist. She pulled out the foil cover, gave one to Sandy, and took one for herself. The smoke sailed between them in a stale, white mist.

"How long have you known Yona?"

"A while."

"Does he know about you?"

"That I'm trans?"

"Yes."

"He's always known."

"Is it difficult between you two?"

"What do you mean?"

"Is it a difficult subject to bring up?"

Sandy shook her head. "No, it's pretty basic for us."

"How did y'all meet?"

"We worked together and noticed each other one night at a club."

"A gay bar?"

"Yeah, it was a gay bar."

"What was he doing there?"

"Trolling for trannies." Sandy grinned at Ama's shocked expression. "I'm just kidding. His friends took him there as a joke and he noticed me from work and we started talking."

"I'm not buying it."

"Buying what?"

"His friends took him there as a joke? I don't buy that for a second. That's bullshit."

Sandy felt heat emanating from her forehead and cheeks. "Okay, he did frequent this bar looking for transsexuals."

"Is he gay too?"

"No...He wasn't sure what he wanted. He liked Trans girls for some reason, but he didn't want a relationship until we met...He isn't sure about himself, and I don't force him to talk about anything. He's happy and that's enough for now."

"Do you have sex?"

"Yeah, we have sex all the time."

"He doesn't care that you have a penis?"

"I don't know. He doesn't talk about it."

"Y'all fuck and you don't talk about it?"

She was hoping she wouldn't ask that. "Yeah, pretty much."

"How does that work?"

"It just happens."

"Like?"

"I'm not gonna talk about my sex life with you."

"Alright," she said. "Does he drink?"

"Yeah, he drinks a little."

Ama blew smoke that fluttered across the dashboard. "I wish he wouldn't. His grandfather drank. How much does he really drink? Is it just a little?"

"He's a beer guy. He drinks a can of beer with his dinners most of the time."

"No whiskey?"

"On special occasions."

"Special occasions? Like every other Wednesday, Christmas, what are we talking here?"

"Now and again. Not very much. I've never seen him get drunk before, so..."

"He should stay away from booze."

"I guess he should, but what's life without a break now and then? You're okay with him smoking."

Ama looked at the burning cigarette in her hands. "The habit was always close to me. I wish I wanted to stop."

"I wish I did, too." Sandy had her own question. "What was it like growing up here?"

"Backwoods," she said. "Every John in town would ignore you for being Indian, and then, when the coast was clear, try to fuck you behind the shed. They all wanted a piece, but all they were gonna get was a knife to the gut."

"You stabbed a guy?"

"No, I never stabbed anybody. But had my knife on me when I was out, and I'd threaten to scream rape."

"I was raped once." She didn't notice what she had said until it was too late.

"When?" Ama asked.

She sighed. "I was young. It was my last year of high school. I went to a club. A guy took me to a bathroom stall and...told me to get over it once he was finished."

Ama didn't say anything. She kept smoking.

"I wasn't really sure if it was rape. I mean, I was into it until I wasn't anymore...you know?"

"Nope," she said bluntly.

"Well, at least I still have a soul."

She continued to steer around the tight corners and through the eerie, creaking steel bridge over the rushing water. Ama finished her cigarette and tossed it out the window. They eventually passed the totaled police cruiser.

"I was in there when it crashed."

"How?"

"I told a cop to help me and Yona, and he put me in the back and drove to the house. The sprouts got him."

"Poor guy."

"They beat him to death with two-by-fours."

"They probably ate part of him too," said Ama.

"Ate part of him?"

"I've seen it a few times. Not an appealing sight."

Sandy began to laugh. It seemed uncontrollable. Her stomach hurt from the tearful bursts of maniacal laughter. She tossed her cigarette butt out the window in case she dropped it from her lips.

"Why's that funny?"

"It's not," she said. "It's just...." She kept laughing.

"What?"

"It's just so fucked up is all."

"Yeah, it's all pretty fucked up," she said, looking ahead. A black truck was parked across the narrow country road, blocking the path.

Sandy felt sick. She pressed the brake and shut the engine off several yards away from the truck. Jack Caulfield leaned against the hood of the car. His attire blended with the vehicle. Two unfamiliar men in similar clothes stood by him like deputies at a police checkpoint. The two men stayed by the car as Caulfield walked toward Sandy and Ama. He moved his hand in a circular motion, wordlessly asking them to roll down her window.

"I could run over him," said Sandy.

"He's probably armed. He'd shoot us through the glass before you could get the engine warmed up. Even if we did hit him, those two guys behind him would keep shooting until the tires were flat and we fell off the ridge here."

"What are you saying? We just roll down the window and talk?"

"No, we neutralize the situation." Ama stepped out of the white truck and walked into the road, meeting Caulfield halfway. They stood face to face and began talking. Sandy couldn't hear them. Their voices were muffled and she couldn't read their lips. It occurred to her that they were speaking Cherokee, which was odd since Jack was from the West. If Sandy hadn't had such an extensive background in linguistics, she wouldn't have thought twice, but she knew that Native American languages from the East and West differed greatly, and it was difficult to pick up an intricate language like Cherokee, especially in a region inhabited by only twenty or thirty fluent speakers. Maybe Ama understood Navajo or Apache? Perhaps they were still speaking English and she couldn't tell the difference? She stared at them and began to sweat, waiting for any possible hand signals from Ama or a sudden barrage of gunfire. Caulfield moved his hands as he spoke. He seemed to be cajoling Ama. It was the way he smiled. Sandy recognized the smile. There was poison in it. Ama pointed to the truck. She seemed to be getting angrier. Sandy turned around and looked at Yona. He was still sleeping. She felt his pulse in his wrist, which seemed normal, tranquil, steady. She looked back at Ama and saw that Jack had stepped a few feet away from her. He was thinking about something, pondering something she had said. He scraped up the chipped remains of a crushed box turtle with his black boots and kicked the brown and green pieces across the road. Sandy pulled her gun from her pocket and placed it in the nearest cup holder. Why did she have to turn the engine off? She could have floored the gas pedal and killed all three of them, then carefully driven to the hospital. She suddenly realized her sedan was still parked in the gas station lot, unless someone had towed it. Whoever was looking for the owner of the car was probably looking for Thatcher too. They probably wanted her for his murder. But who were they? They were probably the powers that be; the man, the government, the racist creators of a flawed capitalist system designed to keep anyone who wanted something different from life down in the gutter. She thought about all this in the nanosecond it took for her to blink, still keeping her attention on Ama and Jack Caulfield. Her right leg shook and her palms were sweaty. She felt like thrashing her skull into the steering wheel, but remained still, almost paralyzed. She watched as Jack laughed and put his hand on Ama's shoulder. She forced it off like he was infected and contagious. She yelled at him. Sandy looked past them and watched the two white guys in all black, standing by the truck. They didn't budge and their faces revealed nothing, no insidious plan, no sadistic intent. Their faces were almost innocent in a bizarre, detached way. Sandy could feel a panic attack coming on. She gripped the steering wheel and, not able to endure another second, started screaming. Ama looked back at her and drew an old revolver from her shirt and fired at Caulfield's face. His head jolted to the side as the smoke blasted over the side of his face. Sandy saw the top half of his ear was gone. Blood poured down his neck as he fell to the ground.

With a loud crack, the tempered glass of the back window nearly shattered. A short figure held a sledgehammer prepped for another swing. It swung at the window again and the streaks of broken glass stretched further, sprouting more branches and detours. Sandy reached for her gun and shot twice through the window. The child fell on its back as the hammer slammed into the metal of the truck bed beside him. He had been shot twice in the chest. Sandy whipped around and started the engine. The two men across the road finally sprang to life and ran after the truck amid the rumble of the diesel engine. Sandy shoved the truck into reverse and floored the gas pedal. The vehicle shot backwards and lashed to the side. Without thinking, she shoved the gear into drive and pressed down on the gas. The truck moved forward and she saw what looked like a tidal wave of foliage, as though a tree branch had fallen on the car. The truck began to thrash like a boat and she realized she had driven off the ridge. The grill crashed into the creek, conforming to the terrain of moss-covered rocks and chipped pebbles. Her airbag erupted from the steering wheel. Shards of glass from the back window spilled over Yona's body.

"What the fuck?" Yona yelled.

Sandy turned to look at him. She couldn't tell whether or not he was worse. He was probably was. She unbuckled and opened her door, crawling out among the wet stones. The boy's body lay in the stream. His hands and legs shook. She laughed. She kept laughing until his elbows curved upward and he lifted himself out of the water. There were still two bleeding wounds in his chest. She ran backwards and tripped, falling to her side. The boy ran after her, his soaked shoes dunking in and out of the shallow water. She didn't have her gun. She looked over to the truck and saw the sledge hammer lying in the mud. There was a rustling coming from the flattened foliage above her. The two men in black were carefully making their way down the ridge. She staggered to the hammer and swung it at the child. A streak of mud flew from the handle as the blunt force knocked the boy a foot to the side. His face plunged into the mud. Sandy raised the hammer and let it fall into the back of his head. She beat down on him as hard as she could, swinging the hammer like a maul or axe. The boy's skull became swollen as blood gushed from the top. The two men grabbed onto her and fought the axe from her hand. She lost her endurance and let herself collapse.

Jack Caulfield yelled from the road. "Bring the girl up here! Then get the Cherokee man in the back. He's wounded! Don't let anything happen to him."

"What about the sprout?"

"Leave it."

As they forced into the black truck, Sandy saw no trace of Ama.

Ama remembered dragging herself through the mud, dragging her body back home in the rain in the spring of 1974. Her muscles were weak. Her skin stung and ached. Jack could never know where her son lived. He would stay on the farm. He was the only reason she was alive. Shortly after that, she discovered the gun in all its simplicity and security. She shot cans lined up on tree stumps. She shot American men in parking lots and Appalachian bars.

Now she was lost. Hidden somewhere in a lightless crypt, feeling herself disappear. Her body was changing.

CHAPTER THIRTY

S he was taken to a large, yet decrepit house on the top of the mountain. The house was barely white, steadily taking on the faint yellow hue of a diseased tooth. Large flakes of the paint shed from the side of the wood paneling.

She didn't talk or ask any questions on the ride, opting to stare at the woods beyond the tinted truck windows. Caulfield parked the black truck in the dirt lot adjacent to a pile of wood, which someone had been chopping down into burnable U shapes. A maul and a hatchet remained sunken into the one of the thicker logs. The two men pulled her out of the car like prison guards transporting an inmate. They kicked open the door to the basement and dragged her through a maze of crumbling yellow-brick catacombs.

"Where's Yona?" she finally asked.

"He'll be fine. He'll be upstairs." They brought him there in the bed of the truck.

She had not seen Ama since she had been pushed into the backseat.

They brought her to a cage-like contraption made of out spare bed frames. A small door flap had been welded onto the side. One of them wriggled a key into the lock and lifted the flap. She was hastily thrown inside. She had nothing more to look at but shadows and the bars of her cage. Everything was held together by flexible springs. She shook the side of the cage. The rusty creaking echoed through the basement. It was loud but completely flexible. She stretched the side of a spring and began unhinging it from the greater metal frame. As a series of footfalls approached her, she relinquished her post and crawled to the far corner of the cage.

An old man in grass-stained jeans and a red polo shirt dragged a stool into the alcove. When he set the stool down and sat, his boney knees extending upwards like crickets' legs, she saw that the object in his hand was a pristine copy of the Holy Bible.

"My name's Llewellyn," he said in a sickly croak. "I'm gonna read sections of the Bible to ya."

She drew closer and noticed his left eye socket was empty. He began to read from Proverbs, reading one line after the other like a series of weak coughs. As he read, he raised his right hand and extended his index and middle finger. She had seen the gesture from innumerable religious icons.

"Who the fuck are you?"

"I'm Llewellyn!" he spat. "I'm gonna read you sections of the Bible." He threw the book on the ground and rattled the spring wall of her cage with his wrinkled, nearly translucent arms. She could see every vein and artery. He returned to the stool and droned on, raising his right hand.

She continued, as clandestinely as possible, to remove the

main springs from the metal frame. Once she removed enough, she could step out of the cage and beat the old man to death with the stool or the hardbound Bible. She listened to his reading and slowly stretched the spring out and wriggled the tip from the hole that connected it to the bed's rectangular frame. She waited for his croaks and coughs to pull out the entire spring cylinder. It was a slow, excruciating process. The ridges of the springs pinched at the web of skin near her thumb while the sharp edges drew blood from her fingertips. She halted as soon as the old man closed the book and laid it on the ground between the stool and the cage like a peace offering. He put his hands on his knees and closed his eyes. He began to recite something from memory. She listened as she kept wriggling the spring from the frame.

"The Bible is the word. The only word. The word of God, frozen throughout time for all men to fear. The Lord is vengeful but forgiving. The eyes of God exist inside the word of God and they are all-seeing. Because they are all seeing, they are all-knowing. Because they are all-knowing, they know the truth of the past, present, and future. All time is, is a circle. God let's everything happen and all that will happen, happen for a reason. God is the sky. The earth. Our blood. He let Christ and countless others be brutally massacred. But God was Christ. And Christ was God. But God was the two thieves behind Christ and the cross he bled on and the nails in his wrists and ankles, and the spear in his side, and the Roman Centurion who stuck it there. God was the people and Judas. God is everything. God is the blasphemer and the killer, the sow and the wolf. The angel and the sinner. The priest and the prophet. All this is God and all things that are God are righteous."

She only had a few pieces to go before she could free herself.

"Everything that he sees he knows will happen. And everything that he knows he forgives. God is forgiveness and forgiveness is the only true God. The pain of the sufferer and the joy of those making the suffering are both God. And God sees and God knows and God allows." His pants and underwear were on the floor now. He masturbated with his left hand. "God is the angry and the violent. The killer and the one gettin' killed. No righteousness can be for not the Lord's decision to make unrighteousness. And he shall be the tempted. And he shall be a temptress: a liquor-mouthed slut, piss-crust in her bed of sin."

She pulled out the last spring. It sounded more like a stone than a ringing piece of metal as it dropped onto the floor and rolled away. She pushed the metal wall outward and crawled under. A sharp piece of steel dug into her back. The old man's eyes shot open. He let go of his penis and grabbed the stool. Sandy freed herself from the cage and kicked his lanky body to the ground.

"You damn whore!"

She grabbed the stool and struck him across his left temple. His head smacked the concrete floor. He tried to push himself up, but she kept striking him with the lacquered seat. The leg finally tore off with an explosive crack. She tossed the splintered wood across the brick cubicle, and walked away, leaving the old man as he writhed on the cold ground. She wiped the blood across her pants as she ran back through the maze. The basement seemed bigger than it actually was with all the poorly made, crumbling walls. She ran into several dead ends where she saw empty dog kennels and rusted cages. There was light coming from somewhere, bright natural light from the world outside. If she followed it she could make it outside. She pulled a piece of paper from her shoe. It was a religious pamphlet. She stopped and thought. She remembered seeing the pamphlets, with their faded blue and yellow ink, in the restaurant with Yona. She walked further down a narrow path, which came to another dead end. A body sat there, propped against brick near a pile of the pamphlets and an empty duffle bag. His throat had been slit open. She ran back through the maze. The walls all looked the same, like dry beeswax mounded to the ceiling. She sat down and caught her breath, rocking back and forth. She knew who she wanted to talk to more than anyone else: her sister. Aileen might not know what to do, but she knew what to say. She remembered calling her when she had begun to transition.

"Really," she had said. "You're sure you're not just gay?"

"This is what I've always wanted, and now I'm not afraid to go ahead and do it."

"This is a very big decision."

"I've talked to a therapist for the past four years at college; I know this is what I want."

"Then do it," she finally said. "When should I start calling you my sister?"

"Anytime you want."

Sandy pushed herself up from the ground and kept walking.

"What should I do, Aileen?"

You know what to do.

"I can't get out of here."

Yes you can. You know the way out. Just keep going.

She took the advice and ran further into the maze, following the light.

Didn't you hear Yona's mom? You're two-spirited, girl. Find the way out on one of those journey things.

"I don't know how to start one. She pushed me off a cliff last time."

You gotta try.

"I don't think I need to." She darted down a wider passage way and turned a corner. The light of the open doorway illuminated the basement and she walked out into the morning sun. Her feet flattened a few brambles as she checked the perimeter of the house. Everyone seemed to be inside, including Yona. She walked back to the lumber pile and stared at the logs. Her hand grabbed onto the hatchet and plucked it from the wood.

Are you gonna be okay? Her sister asked.

"Don't worry, sis." She felt the tip of the blade and hacked at the stump. The hatchet made a perfect notch three inches deep. "Thanks for being here."

I'll stay if you want.

"That's alright. You don't need to see this."

CHAPTER THIRTY-ONE

S andy pressed the doorbell with her thumb. The ring was slow and tinny. A voice from the other side yelled, "Who the fuck is out there?"

"Just a religious woman spreading the good word of neighborly cheer," she said and stepped to the side in case there was gunfire.

A young man with short, black hair pulled the door open and raised a handgun. Sandy sunk the hatchet into the side of his tattooed arm and removed the gun, jamming it into her stained jeans. He screamed at her and she swiped the blade into his throat, leaving him to bleed to death in the open doorway. One of the children leapt from the stairwell on top of her and bit into her arm. She tore the little girl off by her throat and forced her tiny arm onto a nearby table. It took seven hacks before the arm had been completely severed. Shots burst through the kitchen door and she ducked, spreading herself across the floor beside the armless girl's growing pool of blood. One of the blonde men who dragged her to the basement walked in with a double-barrel shotgun under his arm. She shot him once in the chest before he disappeared behind a counter. She stood up and walked into the next room. There were five women in identical dresses with crude, short haircuts, like someone had used hedge clippers instead of scissors. Sweat and snot dripped from their noses as they cowered on the floor in fear. Three of the five were obviously pregnant. She recognized two of them from Nicholas's trailer. They covered their ears with their palms and shut their eyes so tight they seemed to be in pain. Four little boys entered the room. One of them held a baseball bat. She backed away as he swung. Another boy tried to get behind her, but she pushed him to the ground and brought the hatchet down into his chest. Another lunged at her and she kept the hatchet stuck between his neck and his shoulder. Blood gushed over his grimy white shirt. Sandy kept her distance from them as they came closer. The bat slammed into her hip, but she grabbed it from the boy's hands and began swinging with all her might. The remaining three boys were knocked to the ground. Her vision waned as she rotated her body with the bat, beating the children into the carpet. The women screamed and held hands, trying to comfort one another. Sandy closed her eyes and kept beating down with the bat. Her hands were sore from shock when she finally stopped and tossed the bat onto the bodies. One of the women slowly raised her head and looked at her. Sandy looked away and pulled the hatchet free from the boys shoulder. She saw a television across from the couch and turned it on. They went back to hiding their faces from her as Sandy watched a commercial for a used car dealership. She stroked the nearest girl's back. The girl burst into tears.

"I'm not gonna hurt y'all," she said and walked out of the room.

The house became silent. She felt something move behind her.

Her hair stood up. She whipped around, stabbing the wall. She saw nothing. She pulled the blade from the ripped wallpaper and walked up the old stairs. She set the handle of the hatchet through one of her belt loops and took out the handgun. It was heavy and extremely warm. She crouched down on the final steps and held the pistol to the edge of the hallway. The anticipation from the far end of the dark corridor was audible. Someone was breathing, waiting for her to turn the corner. She could have sworn she heard a brief growl as well. As fast as she could, Sandy slid across the rug and pulled the hot metal trigger with her weak index finger. A lone man stood in front of a long mirror at the end of the hall, holding Ama's Winchester. The first bullet grazed the wooden fore end of the gun and ripped off his fingers by the knuckles. The disfigured hand dropped down and the rifle fell to the carpet without rebounding. The next two shots shattered the mirror behind him. The man pressed his weight against the nearest door, trying to open it. She fired once more and the bullet tore through his left temple. Leaving the painfully hot pistol by the steps, she walked down the hallway, heading for the Winchester. The glass crunched under her shoes, slicing into the rubber sole and aged carpet fibers. She picked up the rifle by the leather strap and wiped off the blood with her shirt. There was a barking dog in one of the bedrooms. She kicked the door open. A tall, ribbed Rottweiler lunged at her. She pulled the trigger. The power of the rifle thrashed her against the wall as the wooden butt dug into her sore shoulder. The dog's chest burst. It yelped once before rolling over on the floor and dying. She pulled the leaver and ejected the round. The brass lipstick tube fell next to her seekers, emitting a single waft of clear smoke. She put the lever back, grinding the loose metal and inserting another 30-30 round into the chamber. She checked the bathroom. It was empty. She walked back onto the glistening, broken glass and saw another child in the hallway. He slyly picked up her discarded pistol. The muzzle flash from the Winchester lit up the hallway. The boy's body was propelled several feet back. He managed to shoot the floor before his eyes sank to the back of his head and his jaw lay slack. She kicked open another door to her right and saw an empty room with no furniture. The last unopened door in the hallway was a narrow closet. Three children were hiding underneath a pile of towels. She fired four times and closed the door with her foot.

She squatted down on the hallway carpet and vomited brown stomach acid. After spitting the remnants from her mouth, she lifted her head and sat against the wall, cradling the rifle. Sweat dripped down her matted, salty bangs and seeped into the fibers of her shirt. She heard heavy footfalls coming up the stairs. They were slow, creaking the old wood from the steps. She raised the Winchester for the last time, aimed it at the man, standing before her and pulled the trigger. The rifle was empty, harmlessly clicking like a toy. She threw it to the ground and raised her middle finger.

Jack Caulfield walked down the hallway and looked at the dead man's body, prodding it with his boot. She watched his reflection in the broken flecks of mirror. The partial reflection was not of an Indian man but an indeterminate mass of darkness. His boots snapped a few stray pieces of glass, destroying the image, as he walked back and sat down across from Sandy. The side of his face was badly burned from the gunpowder blast and he wore a bandage neatly wrapped around the hole where his ear had been. Sandy shifted her hand. She was ready to grab the hatchet from her side.

"What's your name?" he asked.

"Sandy."

"Is that short for something, like Sandra?"

"Nope. Just Sandy."

"Just Sandy, do you ever do any gardening?"

She had never been so close to his face before. Despite the scarring, she could see his cherub-like charm coming through. He knew how to carry himself, how to make his self look approachable. He spoke with a soft cadence, suggesting he was younger than he looked. He had Yona's eyes, dark, beady, beautiful.

"No, I've lived in apartments my whole life," she said.

"It has always fascinated me. Agriculture in general, not just gardening. I used to know this farmer who had a big problem with crows always picking his crop to pieces, so he did what every farmer normally does and he set a few more scarecrows in his field. But the crows were a little too smart and kept on eating his crop. He finally went out to the field with a .22 and shot a couple of 'em. The crows behaved in a way he had never seen before. Instead of flying away and finding a safer place to eat, they picked apart their dead and ate them. Now why would they do a thing like that? The farmer was never able to explain. He didn't want an explanation. He didn't want the world to work that way, but he still went out now and then to kill few of the crows so the others wouldn't eat his crop. He just had to live with it."

Sandy inched her hand closer to the hatchet.

"There was a woman, not too far from here actually, who went to church every Sunday, paid her taxes, took care of her kids, let her husband get his rocks off when he wanted, and lived the bare minimum all-American lifestyle we've all dreamed of. But it wasn't enough obviously, it's never enough. She started looking through various websites and advertisements and eventually started selling sex on internet chat rooms to young men in the area. Might be a tad hard to believe in such a drastic change in her behavior, but one assumes she had a soul of slut inside all along. Maybe Uncle Bud stuck his fingers in bad places too often while she was growing up. I think she liked it when twenty-year-olds fucked. Made her feel like she was making up for lost time. Anyway, she kept on doing it on the weekends and certain days when she had time apparently. It didn't take long until one of those young men thought it would be really arousing to shove a power drill up her ass and make her drink at least a gallon of bleach. I doubt her family wanted to know how she really died, so the police here just told them an ex-con killed her by chance. Who could live with that kind of shame, knowing what your wife was doing all day while the kids were at school? But that was the truth."

"Why are you telling me this?"

"These are examples of chance. Who would have thought anything like this would happen? You probably didn't think you had it in you to kill an entire house full of people. But here we are, Sandy."

"Where's my boyfriend?"

"Yona?"

"Where is he?"

"He's downstairs, unconscious, laying on a cot in the furthest room to the left."

"You're lying."

"I'm not," he assured her. "You think I'd let my son die? He's bandaged and we've hooked him up to an IV for now."

"You know he's your son?"

"I've always known. Ama thought she could hide it from me. She thought she was protecting him and her parents. No, I never did anything to hurt him. I stayed away out of respect. Ama could have done a lot more for herself. She's very powerful. At least, she was." He scratched his forehead. "I'm sorry about what happened to Yona. She stabbed him, right? The runaway. I assume that's what happened."

"Her name was Elizabeth."

Jack smiled. "They're all named Elizabeth. That's the moniker we give them. Her real name was Lillian Marie Jones."

Sandy's fingertips brushed the hatchet blade. "Where do you get them from?"

"Believe it or not they join on their own."

"I'm not sure if I do believe it."

"Well...that's life." He rubbed his hands together and wiped them across his black jeans.

"Who are you, Jack?" she asked.

"My name's Jack Eugene Caulfield. I'm from Pocatello, Idaho."

"Ama said you were from the desert."

"I spent a long time in New Mexico, but I'm not from there. My background is Blackfoot. My father died of liver failure when I was nine and my mother was a short-order cook at a diner. I ran away from home when I was thirteen and ended up in a juvenile detention facility until I was seventeen. After that I went to Santa Fe..."

"I don't wanna here your goddamn life story. Just tell me who you are and why you do this."

"What's it matter?"

"Good point." She dove at him with the hatchet. The blade sank into the carpet.

He ran down the hall into the bedroom. She followed him, hoping to get to him before he could get a weapon. She jumped over the dog's body and found Jack, empty handed, standing in the bathroom. He raised his hands, pleading for her to stop.

"Sandy, no, you don't understand."

She hacked into the side of his neck with the blade. A mass of nearly black blood spilled from the gash. She pushed him into the bathtub and raised the hatchet over her head.

"Sandy, you don't...know what you're doing!" he wheezed.

She furiously hacked at his torso, forcing the hatchet down with both hands. He tried to defend himself, but she tore into his arms with deep lacerations until his arms fell to his sides and the tub was smeared with an even layer of red. Finally, she cut into his jeans and severed the femoral artery. His body briefly convulsed and then remained motionless. She spit on the body and turned around.

Jack stood in the doorway, clapping. He was intact aside from the scarring on his face. His grin no longer appeared charming, but cruel, vindictive. He was scum.

"Very good, Sandy," he said. "That was really kind of intriguing to watch. What I'd really like to see is if you have the balls to witness what you've just done."

"You're dead."

"Oh, no. I'm still here. Go ahead, turn around. See what you've done."

"No."

"Oh, come on Sandy. You've come this far."

She slowly shifted to the left until she could see the bathtub.

"There you go, now you've got it," he said.

She sank to the edge of the bathtub, letting the hatchet fall from her hand. She grabbed the mutilated body from the bathtub and held it in her arms.

"Sometimes things get messy, don't they?"

Sandy held Ama tightly and sobbed. She had not seen Ama

there. It was Jack's body, but somehow it was Ama. She rocked back and forth, crying. Her muscles became useless and it felt unable to move. A horrible throbbing sensation emanated from her chest, and her face felt excruciatingly hot. Ama's blood was all over her now. She had done this. She had killed Yona's mother.

"It's not easy is it?"

"How did you do this?"

"Well, it's...it's actually pretty difficult."

"No, no, no." She kept crying, staring at Ama's expressionless face.

Jack pulled the hammer back on his revolver and set it to Sandy's head. "They say you're cursed if you kill a two-spirited person, a Berdache."

She felt the barrel touch her head. She didn't care anymore.

"Don't let anything bad happen to Yona," she said.

"You have my word, for all that it's worth to ya."

She closed her eyes.

"You're biggest enemy ain't black magic or the devil. It's chance."

"Shut the fuck up and pull the trigger!"

The gun fired into the tub, kicking up and barrage of chipped porcelain. A hot piece smacked her cheek. The blast left a strong ringing in her ear. She heard nothing for an entire minute, until she saw the five girls in the bathroom. Two of them held down Jack's arms while the others kept his face submerged in the toilet bowl. He struggled but couldn't break free. The water bubbled and spilled onto the floor.

She finally let go of Ama, gently setting her body in the bathtub. She crossed Ama's arms trying to make her look as peaceful as she could.

Jack finally inhaled, allowing the water to fill his lungs. His boots kicked and stomped on the linoleum. He was granted no final words, no appeal, no moment for an epiphany. He was stamped out like an insect, an unruly wrinkle in fabric. His heart slowed. His brain refused to interpret another sensation. He swallowed one last, heavy gulp and was dead.

The girls prodded his body, making sure he was gone. He remained face down in the toilet water. They turned to Sandy and took her by the hand.

"What are you doing?"

They kept to their submissive vows of silence, and lead her away from Ama and Jack. They clung to Sandy's body as they would a sister, another one like them who could offer comfort and solace, and brought her downstairs.

She didn't need to ask them where she was going. She already knew.

CHAPTER THIRTY-TWO

The girls, all dressed in their identical, drab, gray dress, brought her to a narrow door. She reached out and opened the brass knob. Across from her lay Yona. His body was naked except for the bandages and his arm fixed to a professional IV apparatus filling his veins with necessary fluid. What he needed now was not water but blood. She stepped over to his bedside and, resting on her knees, prodded his shoulder till his eyes opened.

"Sandy."

She leaned over to kiss him.

"Sandy, you're covered in blood."

"It's okay though," she said. "They're all gone."

"I thought I was dead."

"I know."

"You have to get me out of here."

"I will. Don't worry, I will." She turned to the girls standing together, connected by their arms in a giant embrace. "Please, can you bring me a phone?"

The girls headed into the kitchen and brought her a wireless telephone.

"Oh God, thank you. Thank you so much." She gave each one of them a tight embrace and a kiss on the cheek. They accepted her thanks and walked out of the room, closing the door behind them. She kissed Yona one last time and punched in the digits 9-1-1. She held the receiver to her ear and listened....

THE END

Connect with Sandy and Yona online...

Sandra Pogue
Twitter: @PogueSandy
Facebook: on.fb.me/IpmLmv
sandytreeblack@hotmail.com

Yona Bridger
Twitter: @YonaWelds
Facebook: on.fb.me/HK6AET
yonawelds@hotmail.com

A SHORT INTERVIEW WITH CONNOR DE BRULER

Interviewer: What is Tree Black about?
Connor: In the simplest sense, it's about a friendship that's put to the test.

I mean who are the characters?
Oh, I see. You wanna know what happens? There's a difference.

Okay, so what happens?
A transgender woman loses her job in the South because of who she is and her boyfriend, this Cherokee guy, gets blackballed from the same institution. They work at welding school. Anyway, they decide to leave the South. They're ready for new horizons and all. They go up to Appalachia where her boyfriend has the deed to his parents' cabin. Of course, her boyfriend hasn't told her everything about who he is and what's hibernating in the forest.

What's up there in the forest?
Evil. Just pure evil.

Was it a difficult story to write?
No, miraculously this book just kind of fell out of my ass in like four months.

Who are your influences?
Hmmm. I have to say a lot of Southern writers. I'm a big fan of Joe Lansdale, Larry Brown, Harry Crews... I also think the late John O'Brien is the bomb.

Flannery O'Connor?
Nope.

Really?
I liked the movie version of Wise Blood, but I can't stand O'Connor's prose. I don't know why.

Will you write a sequel?
Oh, fuck no.

You had that response on the tip of your tongue.
I don't feel like there's any room for a sequel. I'm eager to write something else.

What advice would you give to other writers?
The best advice I ever heard came from a Youtube video I saw about Stephen King. He said read. You've got to read. You've got

to formulate a style through seeing how others do it. You've got to decide which books you like to read, how you want to read them. What do you want your words to do? Writing is a skill you put time into and figure out how to tell the story you want to tell. You know, it's not something you can do on the weekends and expect to get good at it. I am extremely, emotionally invested in my writing. It's who I am. It's my identity. It has to be the most important part of your life if you want to do it professionally. And don't most of what you hear. People have started writing very late in life and very able to become notable writers: Larry Brown, Bill Buroughs etc. You gotta read and you gotta sit down at the keyboard and just fucking do it.

Thanks for chatting.
My pleasure.

Born in Indianapolis, Connor de Bruler spent the majority of his childhood drifting between different homes and apartment complexes in Greenville, South Carolina. At the age of thirteen his family relocated to Nuremburg, Germany. There, he lived just a few minutes away from the cannibal Armin Meiwes in Rottenburg who was not caught until a year later. He returned to the United States to finish high school.

He currently lives in Rock Hill, South Carolina where he works as a stocking clerk at a grocery and is in the process of finishing his bachelors degree at Winthrop University. He is 21 years old. **Tree Black** is his first published novel.

Printed in Great Britain
by Amazon

38255049R00128